Run With the Hunted 8:
Neural Howlround
By Jennifer R. Donohue

For Jim

Run with the Hunted © 2025 by Jennifer R. Donohue

Ebook ISBN: 978-1-945548-37-6
Paperback ISBN: 978-1-945548-38-3

RUN WITH THE HUNTED 8: NEURAL HOWLROUND3

Chapter One

I'm climbing back down out of the ceiling at Charlie and Lockhart's new arcade when Dolly's pinball machine makes a noise I've never heard before and audibly powers down.

"What was that?" I ask, at the same time as Charlie, who's holding the ladder for me.

"Guess I scored one too many extra balls," she says, laughing and picks up her beer.

"The machine only has—" Charlie starts, and she waves him off with her free hand.

"Trust me, I know," she says when she's finished.

"Why are you playing pinball, anyway?" I ask, zipping up my toolkit.

"Working on my angles."

"From what I hear, you've got that pretty much handled," Lockhart says, going past us with a stack of boxes.

"My reputation precedes me," Dolly says.

"How could it not?" She grins at me and I shrug. "Anyway, everything should be all hooked up and ready now."

"Thanks, Bits, I owe you one," Lockhart says.

"No you don't," I say, and he laughs.

"You can't keep carrying that," he says.

"I probably can," I say.

"I dunno, Bitsy, they didn't have pinball in that one." Dolly slings her arm around my neck. "There's whole arcades that're just pinball, you know."

"Yeah, I do know. It's just funny that it's so important to you now."

"People get new interests all the time. Plus, the old ones are purely mechanical so it gives me a chance to get into their guts, unlike sparky over there."

"It *sparked*?" Lockhart isn't smiling anymore, and Charlie looks skeptical.

"I'm exaggerating." Dolly's smile doesn't slip, but she takes her arm back and lets me finish packing up. "Anyway, it's not as weird as if, like, Bristol got into a shooter or something."

"Okay okay," I say.

Bristol, sitting at the not-yet-opened snack bar, looks up from her phone. "Though, on the topic of games, darlings, do people actually pay real money for currency in these games?"

"Broadly, yes, but what do you mean by these games?" I ask. "Are you playing a *game* on your phone?" I'd assumed she was texting Will. He hasn't been away from her for this long since we kidnapped him, and he'd been kind of anxious.

Bristol sighs. "Yes, I'm playing a game on my phone. Garnet and Suzette *both* sent me invites and then I had an absolutely terrible time choosing which one of them got the credit for my joining."

"The worst," Dolly says, going to crowd in and look at Bristol's screen. "What's the game, one of those matchy-match things? Somebody playing dress up? A bakery?"

"Honestly, Dolly," Bristol says, laughing and pulling her phone back. "That doesn't make me want to tell you."

"Well now I gotta know, is it that embarrassing?" Dolly fake-grabs at her phone, and I say fake-grabs because if she meant it, Bristol couldn't beat her.

"No it's not *embarrassing*," Bristol says, and I wonder why her cheeks are getting pink. "It's about *archaeology*."

Dolly stops grabbing. "It what."

"Oh, are you playing The Dig?" I ask.

"Yes! Yes, The Dig." Dolly still looks blank, and comically surprised. "It's something of a puzzle game, I suppose, where you can choose the means by which you excavate an archaeological dig, but then you also decide upon the documentation of the objects you unearth, and *then* whether they're sold on auction, sent to a museum, whether the site is maintained in situ, it's all very involved." She looks from me, to Dolly, who doesn't seem elucidated. "But you have to pay your experts and workers and such, and I've just been using the in-game means to earn the currency but there is the option to spend real money on it, which I simply don't understand."

"Pay to win, Bristles, a tale as old as time," Dolly says, finally laughing. She reaches across the snack bar to put her empty bottle in the sink. "I just never thought I'd see the day."

"It isn't as though I've never played a game before," Bristol says.

"No, but I would've taken you for one of those pie shop games or something, but about a fashion house. Does that exist? If it doesn't exist, Bits should make it, and we'll make money hand over fist. Build a fashion house from scratch and you gotta make designs and get into shows and stuff. I dunno."

"We don't need to make money hand over fist," I point out.

"Yeah, but who doesn't like diversifyin' their income streams." Dolly picks up her jacket off one of the stools and shrugs into it. "So you're digging up a pharaoh or something?"

"Well I'm not certain yet what this particular dig is, it might be a rich merchant's tomb."

"*Have* you dug up a pharaoh? How long have you been playing this game behind our backs?" Dolly winks at me, and I raise my eyebrows at her. Like, yeah this is a little weird, but she's really grabbing onto it.

"It isn't behind your backs, you never ask what I'm doing on my phone." Bristol drops her phone in her purse and stands up. "Only a few weeks, I suppose. I've also sent Marquis an invite, but they've been busy. Also Suzette is busy planning her wedding, so I'm not certain how she's quite so advanced as she is."

"Unless she's buying currency?" I ask, to stave off the inevitable wedding talk, and Bristol nods.

"The plot thickens," Dolly hoots.

"Thanks again, Bits," Lockhart says, coming behind the bar to get himself a beer.

"Tell me if you have any problems," I say. "Don't just go up there with a pair of pliers and roll of wire and think you'll fix it yourself."

"He won't," Charlie says. "I made sure that the ceiling isn't big enough for either of us." Lockhart punches his arm, and they both laugh.

"We'll try not to get this one shot up," Dolly says.

Charlie tries this time. "Guys, we already said—"

"Look, when we leave a wake of destruction, we like it to be on purpose, not just incidental," Dolly interrupts with a grin. "So can it."

He holds up his hands. "Fine, I surrender."

"What do you mean 'when you leave a wake of destruction?" Lockhart asks. "Did you get somebody else's private exclusive arcade full of vintage cabinets shot up in a different city?"

"Nah, nothing like that," Dolly says. "Actually, I guess we keep pretty clean margins. Even at the end of the Vegas game it was pretty neat."

"It was," I agree. We don't talk about Morocco. "But we work together much better by now." And I don't make those kinds of mistakes about how our devices might be tracked. The diamonds job didn't need to go as wrong as it did.

"Well, we look forward to not being collateral again." Charlie takes Lockhart's beer. "Take care of yourselves."

"We always do," Dolly says. Bristol has her phone out again and is looking at it, instead of engaging in the chatter, which is a little odd, but I keep my eyes to myself for now.

I didn't need to, because once we're outside, she shoves her phone at me. "See! Look at Suzette's profile."

I look; in The Dig, you can see your friends' profiles in more detail than just any other player, and so Bristol can view things like assets and staff, and the date each dig starts. Suzette *does* have a lot of the currency, and while I'm sure somebody who's obsessed and hyperfocused could get that much in game, she's obviously spent a lot of money instead. Like it or not, I'm privy to a lot of the wedding planning, from how I handle the security of our devices, and also of all the ordering and preparations that Nicolai and Suzette are doing. "But it's built right into the game, right? She isn't cheating," I say. I actually don't know why it bothers Bristol, who is never one to ignore an advantage.

"No, she isn't cheating," Bristol says. "I just don't know why you would buy something that isn't *real*."

"You're tellin' me that if you could like, spend cold hard cash to buy, I dunno, a Fabergé egg in that game and that was the only way you could get it, you wouldn't?" Dolly asks, lighting a cigarette.

"I am saying that, yes." Bristol takes her phone back.

"Wild." Dolly tries, I think, to blow a smoke ring, but it's too windy.

"No, I get it," I say. Bristol is about appearances, sure, but she's *materialistic*, literally. She doesn't buy knockoffs of things, she buys the real things. Like when she wanted those red soled shoes.

"Thank you, Bits," Bristol says. She stops again, sends a message.

"You know, Bristol, it's real hurtful that you didn't send invites to either of us. No no, it's fine, don't send one now. It'll be because I asked, not because you want me to play."

"I assumed you'd be bored to tears," Bristol says. "You really ought to be thanking me for taking your feelings into consideration rather than imposing my expectations upon you."

"Oh I'm thankful," Dolly says. "Except, the thing is, now..."

"Now we need to talk about what you girls are wearing to Nicolai and Suzette's wedding!" Bristol says happily.

"The other shoe," Dolly says to me, and I sigh.

Chapter Two

Beach towns are great places for arcades, apparently, but can also be great places for wedding clothes shopping. Destination weddings, maybe? It isn't the kind of thing I devote a lot of time or thought to, but Bristol won't just let me wear my bodyguard suit from her wedding that wasn't. You can't rewear wedding outfits, apparently, whether they're fake or not.

"Plus, there's the matter of your plus one," she says. "I'm bringing Will, of course—"

"Poor guy," Dolly says, and grins at Bristol when she gets A Look™. "And I'm bringin' Butler of course. What about Marquis, are they attached?"

"They have choices they can make," Bristol says cryptically.

"I wasn't going to bring a...anybody," I say. I don't want to say 'a date,' that isn't something I'm interested in. "I assumed I was going to be spending most of it in VR making sure of all the security. With the people we know, that's kind of important."

"Well that ain't very fun," Dolly says, and I shoot her a look. I don't need her taking Bristol's side in this. "Weddings are for all those dumbass activities that the DJ makes everybody do, and the bouquet toss and garter toss and chicken dance and stuff."

"The chicken dance is a group dance, I don't need a plus one for that."

"I'm not certain that the chicken dance is something we shall see at an international wedding such as this," Bristol says with careful disdain.

"Yeah, that might be. It's an oldie anyway, I'm surprised it isn't retired by now. Put out to pasture. Or...bucket? Soup. You stew old chickens."

"Dolly." Bristol's tight voice and bright smile are *very* clear.

"Are you hopin' to catch the bouquet, Bristol?" Dolly asks, smiling sweetly. "You know I won't line up for it, bein' a married woman and all."

"I do forget that," Bristol says with studied carelessness. "What is Butler occupying himself with just now, that he can't be here with us?"

"Moonin' around about not being Nicolai's best man. He's pathetic, really, just a joke of a man." Dolly stubs out her cigarette and drops it in a bin. "No, him and Nicolai's brothers are getting the bachelor weekend ready."

"Oh indeed."

"Aren't you Suzette's maid of honor? Should you be with her right now?" Dolly asks, as though she's coming to a sudden realization.

"Trying to get rid of me so soon, darling? The bachelorette party is next week, which you well know, and I scheduled this weekend specifically to make sure that you two will be presentable for the ceremony and reception."

"And here I thought you scheduled this weekend specifically to watch Bitsy run internet cable for her pals while I stood around lookin' threatening. And playing pinball."

"Things can be more than one thing," I say.

"Right like how shopping can also be torture."

"It is not torture," Bristol says, laughing. "Now, I know neither of you care what you look like at the wedding, but I care, and Suzette cares." She pauses, then says, "Possibly Butler does as well."

"Butler doesn't care what Bits wears," Dolly says, grinning.

"That isn't—" Bristol starts.

"He's got respectful opinions on what you wear," Dolly adds, still grinning.

"Well that's very nice of him," Bristol says.

"Far be it for me to keep you from shopping, though," Dolly says. "I need to figure out the wedding present still. What do you get the arms dealer who has everything?"

"Arms and caviar dealer," I say.

"Oh, I forgot about that. Did he tell you about that, Bristles?"

"He did, yes. And provided samples."

"What a guy Nicky is. And I dunno what Suzette likes, I assume the same stuff as you. I could just get 'em gift cards, money's always the right size."

"Suzette and I share a lot of the same taste, yes." Bristol glances towards me in appeal and I shrug.

"I got wine glasses," I say. "They're hand blown glass from some shop in Venice. It seemed like something that she could use."

"That's very thoughtful," Bristol says, sounding almost surprised enough to be insulting.

"I didn't even look at her browsing history or anything," I say.

"You could've looked at the wedding registry," Dolly says, but like she just thought of it. She pulls out her phone. "Bris-

tol'd never do something like that, of course, far too imperson-
al."

"I never said—"

"Just let me give you the compliment, Bristles."

"Fine, then." Bristol pulls out a compact mirror and checks
her makeup, which isn't ever any different from the last time
she looked at it.

Nicolai texts me then. //Very sorry, Bits, are you busy?//

//Yes but not really, what's up?//

//My mother's friend has the necessity to hire somebody,
and my mother thought your abilities might be of use.//

//Me personally or the three of us?//

//Both.//

//Hire somebody for what?//

//To get her niece, Lydia, out of a situation. She's got some
employees who can come out wherever you are, to talk.//

I pause, trying to think of how to word my exact question
without going overboard. //Employees? About her niece?//

//It's a family business.//

Oh, organized crime. //Let me talk to Bristol and Dolly
and get back to you.//

"Nicolai can put us in touch with somebody who's got a
job," I say.

"Nicolai can?" Dolly asks, eyebrows up.

"A friend of his mother. Who has some employees in the
family business that they can send me to meet."

"Gotcha," she says. "Bristles?"

She considers a moment. "I suppose we might as well hear
them out. It might be something we can fit in, right?"

"It might, yeah. He said she needs somebody to get her niece out of a situation."

"Well hell, an exfil can just take a couple hours, no sweat."

"I'm actually wild to hear more, if nothing else," Bristol says. "This seems perhaps outside our usual."

"Okay. Wait a sec and I'll tell Nicolai."

//We'll meet,// I send.

//Thank you, Bits. And my mother thanks you as well.//

//I'll send you our location. Bristol is picking out what Dolly and I are wearing to your wedding.//

//That's certain to be an experience.//

//Can you tell how excited I am?//

//Your excitement clearly cannot be contained.// A few seconds later, an unknown contact pings me their current location and I acknowledge. A couple of hours away, but I know for a fact that Bristol can spend an unlimited amount of time shopping.

"They'll be a little while," I say.

"Perfect, we can continue on then."

Dolly lights a fresh cigarette. "Anyway, Bristol, you keep putting off saying what you got the couple-to-be. Are we gonna track down another lost Fabergé egg for them, would that have enough of a personal touch?"

"It would, but there isn't a convenient one that I'm aware of," Bristol says, glancing at me.

"No, me neither," I say. "Sorry."

"Store bought is fine," Dolly says, as if to herself, and laughs. "Well and you're not gonna make one, so I guess you'll need to pick something else."

"Which I'm hardly likely to find here."

"But you're fine clothes shopping here?"

"For you and Bits, yes."

"But not yourself?"

"You know the answer to that, Dolly darling," Bristol says. "Besides the fact that the bridesmaid gowns are already selected and ordered and I'm to pick mine up in the middle of next week."

"Is it from your pet seamstress in Paris?"

"It is not. Though Suzette *did* consult with her both for those and her wedding gown, she ultimately decided to go elsewhere at her recommendation."

"Why are weddings always in the spring, anyway? Is that some weird symbolism?"

Probably not so weird, but I don't say anything.

"Good heavens, Dolly, I couldn't say."

"Well you're the one I ask this girly stuff," she says.

"And I'm sure I appreciate that, but I haven't got all of the answers. I'm flattered you might think that, though."

"Well I can have Bitsy look it up online but it isn't as fun for anybody, right Bitsy."

"Right." Funny that she says that right as I'm sending a couple of automatic tracking programs after that geotag.

"Regardless, the store is just here. Now, I promise it won't be as bad as you seem to think it will."

"Don't make promises you can't keep," I mutter.

Chapter Three

I hole up in a dressing room to do some research. I don't want to cross any lines and get my fingers in Nicolai's mother's devices, but if you're like me, you can find a lot out about a person just from having their phone number and location. Nicolai's mother is in Russia, the guy's device is Russian, and I pretty immediately get into the information that this phone number was part of a bank of phone numbers purchased at once. Bunch of burners, everybody's known what that means since the late twentieth.

Dolly, for once, humors Bristol as she goes through the dresses and holds things up to consider, and either hangs them back up without comment or hands them to Dolly to take to the dressing room and try on.

"I dunno if that shade of pink is the right one for me," Dolly says at one point. Because I'm in the dressing room, I hacked into the shop's network and accessed the cameras, which have audio. Not all security cameras do. I glance over, and it is *very* pink, not quite fluorescent, that would be 'gauche' to Bristol, but really bright and deep.

"You just think pink is too girly," Bristol says smoothly. "Please try it, the style is lovely."

"We could always chuck it in the bathtub with some dye," Dolly says, finally accepting the hanger.

"Or pay a professional, but yes. Which color would you prefer?"

"You askin' me my favorite color, Bristles?" Dolly asks. It's her teasing tone but there's something else in it that I don't really get. I can see Bristol's face, but not hers, and Bristol's face is almost always the mask she puts on for the world, so I go back to my datastream, still listening.

"I suppose I am. It's actually horrible of me that I never have before, isn't it, darling?"

"Yes and no, you prob'ly thought it'd be an invitation for me to introduce you to the deep and wide world of camouflage."

"Hmm, no, I didn't think that because I never think of camouflage at all." I hear Dolly's laugh, and look up for the smile Bristol put on for that.

"You really should, textiles and patterning for military use are a whole industry unto itself. Plus we know about the advances in active camo. Little box you carry versus fibers in the fabric, and all that."

"While I appreciate the special attention that goes into that, Dolly darling, it is simply outside of my interests. Other than the little box, as you say."

"What's yours?"

"Pardon?"

"Your favorite color."

"I suppose it depends on the season," Bristol says, and that's when one of my datacrawlers pops up with the mined list of special items in The Dig, and how many of them have populated. I set that to run against transactions in both real currency and in-game and check the cameras outside, just out of habit, but the street is clear.

"Here, Bits, we picked these two out for you and this mountain for me, so you can take your time," Dolly says from outside the door. I reach out and nudge it open with my toe as I push my headset up, and she reaches in to hang up a suit that might as well be my bodyguard suit, and a blue dress. "She tried to restrain herself for you, anyway."

"I just had to seize the opportunity, Dolly, *you* understand," Bristol says, smiling. "This may be the only time I ever see you in something other than the extremely safe things that you pick."

"Safe?" Dolly looks at her. "Are you sayin' that I'm, what...afraid to take risks?"

"Fashion risks, yes, obviously. *Other* risks, perish the thought. I would never question your courage."

"Bits, she's tellin' me I'm too much of a coward to wear pink, I just know it."

"And if I am?" Bristol smiles sweetly.

"It's really pink, Bristol," I say. It's making me think of something that I can't really place. The flowers somewhere, maybe.

"It's *lovely*, and if Dolly doesn't scoop it up I might take it for myself." Bristol looks at me, tilts her head just slightly. "Oh, shoes."

"We can worry about shoes someplace else," Dolly says. "We better get this show on the road."

They go to the next dressing room over, and at first I just hear Bristol still in the hallway and then Dolly says "These god-damn zippers are a trap" and the door opens and closes again.

I look at the clothes Bristol picked for me, glance at my programs. Things are running, I can change and change back really quick. I'm trying to think if I ever told Bristol that I like blue, but I can't remember. I'm pleasantly surprised that the blue dress is a jumpsuit that I can pretty much just step into and then do something with a belt. The sleeves are loose and stop around my elbows, and the pants are wide and even with my normal shoes, they'd be the right length. I look at myself in the dressing room mirror for a second, frowning, turning this way and that. It's comfortable enough, it looks fine I guess. Maybe the real surprise is that Bristol thinks a jumpsuit is dressy enough for a wedding, but I don't care in the first place. The suit, I don't bother with. I have a suit, and it's better than this because it's made out of the dragonscale fabric. Though now that Dolly's actually been shot in the dragonscale, we know that it's not the miracle we thought it was.

But we don't talk about that. After enough time passed, I realized that we weren't going to talk about it *at all*. Bristol has never asked me, and I don't know what, if anything, Dolly's said to her about it. She mentioned her being shot quota and we all just glossed right over it like we normally would. Dolly gets shot sometimes, yeah, normal. She doesn't really seem to mind it, which is an insane thing to think, but she's a supersoldier and we aren't, so that makes it make sense.

I think I'd be mad if I was getting shot regularly on behalf of the group. I think I'd be *really* mad if I got shot rescuing Bristol's boyfriend that she only kind of cares about, like a trinket that she keeps around to look at sometimes. To have on her arm sometimes, like this wedding.

That's a funny question; does Bristol care more about Will than her Fabergé egg, or less? The same?

But then Dolly's knocking on the dressing room door again. "Yeah?"

"Bristol found something she thinks is good enough for me, so we're gonna go find food. Nothing shoes is gonna be up-scale enough for her here."

"Okay." I stand up and start to leave, but Dolly doesn't move. "The blue thing," I say.

"It's a good color," she says.

"I like blue." I used to go by Blue, actually, but it's never come up. My at-home, training wheels, learning how to hack handle.

"You like colors in general, I think," Dolly says, going up to the front with an armful of clothes. Bristol's straightening her hair in the hall mirror when I come out to follow her.

"It fits properly?" she asks. "If it doesn't, we have time to fix it now."

"Yeah, it fits." It wasn't too small, anyway. How were things like that supposed to fit. She takes my word for it, though.

"Get any more intel, Bitsy?"

"Not really. I did some snooping, recreationally, but nothing interesting or exciting."

"Fair enough."

Bristol finishes making best friends with the shopgirl and then getting restaurant recommendations, and we're off again.

As we walk, I download The Dig and poke around at it, listening with one ear to Dolly's banter. It wouldn't be all that hard to make and add items for it, I don't think, but it would all depend on their systems. And with a pay to win game, the items wouldn't typically be a vulnerability, the microtransactions would.

"Dolly, while I very much appreciate your trying to take an interest—" Bristol says at one point, and I tune back in.

"Who says I'm tryin' to take an interest?" Dolly laughs. "I think it's *genuinely* interestin' that the biggest statue of a fork and knife are in Kentucky. Though that biggest statue of a pierogi they got up in Canada has a fork with it, dunno if we have a fork off or not."

"Be that as it may, I'm certainly unaware of where in the world the largest pair of scissors would be, and whether there's a *statue* of gigantic scissors or not."

"Well."

Chapter Four

W e're the only customers at the restaurant, in the post-lunch-pre-dinner hours, and they even look surprised when we walk in like, oh yeah right, customers can happen at any time the door isn't locked. But they do seat us, and bring us water and menus and a bread basket, which wasn't really expected in a casual sort of modern-ish fish and chips kind of place.

Dolly grabs bread immediately, then shoves the basket closer to me. Bristol sips her water and looks at her phone. "How much longer until our guests?" she asks, and I check my tracker.

"Probably another half hour, forty five minutes."

"Anybody got a deck of cards?" Dolly grins.

"We could go back to the arcade if you're *that* bored, darling."

"Nah, this is good practice."

Practice for what? Bristol doesn't ask, so I don't either.

"There's some kind of game in the hallway by the bathrooms," I say. Something in a cabinet to look old fashioned, but looks like it's connected to a cloud subscription of games.

"Oh well there's that," Dolly says, and goes to look.

Bristol sighs slightly and orders a bottle of white wine. Eventually, I order dessert, to draw things out. It's funny that Bristol and I are each happy to occupy ourselves with our devices, but in such different ways. She's playing The Dig but she's also chatting with a number of people, singly and in groups. I don't look at who. Dolly comes back for her drink, and to drag me to see the video game setup. It's what I guessed it was from the connection, but the cabinet is nice. Everybody always loves arcade cabinets.

The tracker keeps me updated and then, eventually, they're in town, and then down the street, and then walking in.

They look around, also expecting other people to be here. When they see us looking at them, the bigger of the two shrugs and just walks over. "We didn't mean to keep you ladies waiting."

"Be our guests," Bristol says, as a member of waitstaff scurries for more water glasses and menus and another bread bowl to put in front of our *guests*.

"Well this is awkward," the shorter one says, perched nervously next to Dolly and trying to laugh.

"Everybody's got a first time," Dolly says.

"Let's make some introductions," Bristol interrupts. "Obviously, you seem to know who *we* are, Mr...."

"Don't bother with mister, just call him Johnny and I'm Ringo."

"Very well." Bristol picks up her wineglass; she ordered a bottle of white that Dolly's ended up helping her with.

Ringo starts to speak and then the waiter comes back for their orders, and then somebody refills our waters, and then their food is brought out. We all take a near-comedic pause after that, to see what else will show up, and when it isn't anything, that's when Ringo finally starts talking.

"Okay, so I'm not going to screw around, we want to hire you. Nicolai's mother is very admiring of you. Plus, we know about the diamonds job, and we know a little bit about what went down in Morocco. As much as anybody knows what went down in Morocco."

"Nicky doesn't know when to shut the fuck up," Dolly says, still grinning.

"And our reputation has led you to think that we are the best team for your job?" Bristol asks.

"Your reputation makes us think that you're the *only* team for our job," Johnny says. "If we want the right people to stay alive."

"I see." Bristol glances at me.

"Why don't you tell us the job, and we'll talk about it," I say. I understand the need for all this discretion but also there's a point at which all the cagey talk means nobody's saying *anything*.

"We need you to find somebody," Johnny says. "And bring her to us."

Bristol reacts immediately, setting her glass down so hard it sloshes a little. "Kidnapping? No."

Ringo holds up his hands. "No, no, it's not kidnapping it's...more of a rescue. She's in with the wrong kind of folks, and being fed the wrong kinds of ideas. We think she's going to need deprogramming."

"You understand how it sounded," Bristol says. She isn't out of her chair yet, but she isn't apologizing either.

"Sorry, my way with words is. Bad." Johnny grimaces.

"That's why I was supposed to do the talking," Ringo says, but he doesn't seem mad. Just tired. "We're prepared to make a very generous offer. The boss is very fond of her niece."

"Sure," Dolly says. "And very unfond of who her niece's hangin' out with, we get that. What do you mean when you're talking about deprogramming, though? This some kinda cult?"

"It's a group of newer money venture capitalists and socialites, and yeah, they've got a weird sort of cult. It's not around a person, though, it's some kind of AI."

"How is such a thing possible?" Bristol says. "If it's not a person..."

"I've heard about these kinds of things," I say, because of course I have. Even with the shitty AIs back in the twenties, people were doing things like this. "There are still going to be people who are important in the structure of the cult, whoever *runs* the AI or whatever. But they claim it all centers on the AI."

"So what do you even do about that?" Dolly asks. "Hit it with hammers?"

"It's decentralized," I say, and Dolly makes a disappointed face. "Much as you like hitting computer stuff with a hammer."

"It's real fun."

"We don't care about the AI, we just care about Lydia. The niece," Ringo says.

"But could we increase our fee if we take care of the AI?" Dolly asks.

"We aren't in a position to negotiate that," Ringo says. Johnny's texting under the table, but I don't say anything and he doesn't say anything. It makes it so easy when they're sitting next to me, to follow the ping, and then actually copy the packet. It's a terrible breach of a person's privacy to read their texts, but also I need to know if they're telling the truth about wanting to hire us, or if this is a plan to get us someplace and gun us down or whatever. Johnny really is asking the contact if there would be an addition to our fee if we take care of the AI, and that's a pleasant surprise. It's not like we can *trust* these guys, necessarily, but we probably won't need to trust them to do anything but pay us.

I look up and Dolly's gaze flicks to me for the time it takes me to raise my eyebrows a little, to mean yes, as I reach for my water.

"Alright, so why can't you just go get her?"

"We've done that. Twice. She just goes back to them. And now we don't know where she is, they're yachting around the world or some other bullshit." Ringo glances at Bristol. "Excuse me."

"Thank you, it's all right." What a funny thing for him to do. Apologizing for cursing? Bristol looks at me, and then at Dolly. "What do we think, girls?"

"Well, it's been awhile since I exfiltrated somebody at sea, but that's not something you really forget how to do, right?" Dolly asks, and then laughs at the various looks on our faces. "Yeah, I think it's something we could do."

"Agreed," I say. I'm actually really interested in getting into the guts of the so-called AI, but I'd do that for free. Especially since I don't think it's actually going to be an AI, since I've never seen one that's any better than a glorified chatbot. I'm not holding my breath. "And it won't be that hard to find the yacht, I don't think."

"You could call Nautical Deborah," Dolly says.

"That's true." I probably don't need to, but I can admit that having connections is good and useful. Beneficial. "But we don't need to get into that here."

"So you're taking the job?" Ringo asks. Johnny looks up from his phone; he's been waiting for an answer, none received yet. So he isn't texting the boss, then, he's texting to somebody who will ask the boss themselves and then relay the intel.

"Yeah, we'll take the job," Dolly says.

Johnny's phone pings at the same time Bristol's does, and she fishes hers out of her purse as he puts his on the table. "We can pay you more for the AI," he says. "It's probably not on the boat."

"I'm not worried about that," Dolly says. "That's what Bits is for. Well, and the deprogramming, I guess, you're gettin' pretty good at that."

"If I had a nickel for every person I've deprogrammed, I'd have two nickels. Which isn't a lot, but it's weird that it's happened twice." Dolly brays a laugh, louder than the first one, and I grin. Bristol cocks her head just a little, amused but not *that* amused. The men just look confused but they're used to operating on a need-to-know basis, obviously. "So how do we contact you?" I ask, like I don't already own their devices and have access to their mothers' doorbell cameras. "The number Nicolai gave me?"

"No, this number," Ringo says, sliding his phone over as he gets an alert for The Dig. The noises for that game are interesting, I'm not sure they're electronic at all or if they're actually real recorded sounds. It's so old-fashioned, for a phone game. Very analog.

"Excuse me, are you also playing The Dig?" Bristol asks, another surprise.

"You've gotta be kidding me," Dolly mutters, kicking back in her chair.

"*You* play The Dig?" Johnny asks, his mouth actually hanging open. "I thought somebody like you would—"

"Yeah we just went over this like two hours ago," Dolly says. "Who knew you'd be such a nerd, Bristol."

"We *did* already go over this," Bristol says, smiling indulgently. "And I do think maybe I didn't get to explain that some of the artifacts are based on real ones? One might choose to dig a known historic site or one procedurally generated."

"No, you explained somethin' like that," Dolly says. "I think."

"Dolly doesn't play phone games," Bristol says to the table at large.

"Can you even play phone games, or do you just see floatin' code?" Dolly asks me.

"It depends," I say. "Sometimes I do just want to play solitaire or one of those matching the tiles mahjong games or whatever."

"Solitaire! There are so many games in the world, and you want to play solitaire."

"Sometimes I'll even play it the old fashioned way, with real playing cards."

"What can you do with people like this," Dolly asks the men. They kind of shrug, and look back and forth between themselves and us.

"Can we...friend you on the game?" Ringo asks.

"Oh I suppose so," Bristol says, and as they get their phones together to do that, Dolly rolls her eyes and orders a beer.

Chapter Five

When we get to the hotel, I ping Nautical Deborah about the yacht. We might need our own yacht, I think. Boat of some kind. How does one get onto an exclusive AI cult yacht? I don't want Dolly to decide to prove how far she can swim or something like that. I'm sure she knows, actually.

Bristol and Dolly are bickering about...something...and Nautical Deborah gets back to me almost immediately.

//ahoy there, stranger!//

//Is now a good time?//

//there are no bad times, Bits, what's going?//

//well I need to ask you about a yacht, and a yacht.//

//Okay, which yacht first?//

//We need to find a target yacht, so that one first. Apparently they're an AI cult// I send her the intel on the niece, and on the people she was last known to be associated with.

//oh weirdoes like that are always fun!! Please hold.//

I slide up my headset and Dolly breaks off what she was saying and looks at me. "Finding the yacht first," I say. "And then find our possibilities."

"I mean, dependin' on where they are, we can just take a helo out there and grab her," Dolly says.

"You've always wanted to fly a helicopter on one of our excursions," Bristol says.

"Yeah, and I couldn't the last time because I was in charge of the dog." Dolly takes a thoughtful sip of her beer. It's a can I don't recognize, either she had it in her bags somewhere or there's a vending machine nearby. "Think her hair came back in okay?"

"Whose? The *dog's*?" Bristol asks. "I have no earthly idea."

"It probably has," Dolly says. She looks at me and I shrug. "What, you never wonder about what we leave in our wake?"

"Not a whole lot," I say.

"No," Bristol says.

"Well now that's a lie, Bristles, look at Will." Bristol sighs as Dolly laughs, and takes her beer.

"Yes, look at him. He's still got such potential, n'est-ce pas?" She takes a sip, and it's only because she's Bristol that she doesn't make a face, even I can see that. "Honestly, Dolly, we have *so* much money..."

Dolly takes the can back. "Aw, you just don't like beer." She looks at me, and lowers her voice theatrically. "It's real bad beer, but there's a comfort in that, y'know?"

"If you say so," I say, and then Nautical Deborah pings me again and I lean back in the armchair and slide my headset back down again.

//Okay, Bits, looks like your target was most recently in Sri Lanka and is heading North West, which is good.//

//Why is that good?//

//Well it means that they're not heading south west, towards one of most prevalent areas of rogue waves on the *planet*.//

//That would probably cut the job short, yeah.//

//Exactly! Anyway they kind of seem to be doing kind of a figure eight? Either they go from Sri Lanka through southeast Asia, or they go northwest up to the Med. Mostly the Med, actually.// She sends over the map with the location pings, from satellite and buoys and channel markers and stuff. //The boat's registered name is Pandora's Box.//

//That makes the Mediterranean make a lot of sense. Anywhere near your seastead at any point?// I'm still not exactly sure where it is. I haven't needed to know, and in this case, my idle curiosity wasn't reason enough. Hacker's honor or whatever.

//Nope, much as we'd like to have you out and use us as a staging area, it wouldn't be useful! Looks like your best bet might be Greece? Italy? Turkey? Though they don't go up the strait to Turkey very often either.//

//They could probably be nudged.// I zoom in on that area, but it's not really small enough to be an effective trap. //Venice maybe.//

//It's hard to say why they set the headings they do, it's not seasonal.//

//Maybe the AI is telling them to go that way and that's why it's spiralling/figure eighting like that.//

//Oh that would make sense.// She sends over a couple more maps, more specific charts of the leadup into Venice and then the lagoon itself, the strait that leads up to Istanbul (not Constantinople).//Do we have any idea how AI the "AI" for the AI cult is?//

//Zero clue.//

//Sure would be something if this turned out to be a real one.//

//It would, but it'd be a big surprise.//

//Leading us to think it's still a no.//

//Exactly.// She sends me another data packet, so I can access the satellites that she's been using. //Thanks for all the help.//

//Anytime, Bits! I'll let you know if I come across anything else that might be helpful.//

//I really appreciate that.//

This time when I slide off my headset, Dolly's sitting on one of the beds and Bristol is in the bathroom. From the sound of it, the tub is filling, and from the smell of it, somebody bleached the tub first. "You want a beer?"

"No, thanks." I stand up and stretch, tired but wired. "So the yacht's been taking a sort of predictable pattern and we can decide what to do based on that. Yacht or helicopter or not even going out to sea at all."

"Are you really gonna miss an opportunity to go out to sea?" Dolly grins.

"Yes? I don't know if I'd want to do it with an unwilling participant who I then have to deprogram."

"Okay yeah, fair." The beer Dolly has now is different. Maybe better quality? Who can say. "Are you gonna be able to do that? Cult 'programming' is a lil different from what me and Will had."

"I think that even though the sources are different, the principles are the same. I'll know once I talk to her, though. Or spend time with her social media history, which I haven't done yet. Sometimes families think that somebody must be brainwashed when really they just want to live their own lives." I roll my head back and forth until my neck pops. All chairs are not created equal, and I think back to my time in Mexico, the immersion chair and node all to myself. It's not like I have trouble getting a connection ever anymore, both from my own personal upgrades and also the way global connectivity capabilities keep improving.

"Yeah, there's that. Wonder what we'll do if that's the deal, Bristol bein' how she is."

"I can hear you, darlings," Bristol calls from the echoey tub. Dolly laughs. "Yeah I know."

"We'll burn that bridge when we come to it, same way we always do."

"Y'know, I think we've burned few things, now that I'm thinkin' about it."

"We do have a sense of self-preservation," Bristol calls.

"What're you in the tub for if you're gonna keep talkin' to us?"

"Well I didn't know Bits would be done already, I don't want to miss anything." Some sloshing, as Bristol exits the tub, and then she pulls the bathroom door open and appears in a fluffy hotel robe. "How'd you find her so quickly, darling?"

"Nautical Deborah helped cut the time," I say.

"Some day, you must tell us how you met her," Bristol says. She sits on the arm of Dolly's chair. And I watch Dolly shift without really shifting, and finish her beer, setting the can on the little table with the others. "Are you able to tell where the yacht is now?"

"Yes, I've got an eye on it now, and before I go to sleep I'll write a script to track where it goes, and to capture faces if people disembark. They don't register travel plans with anybody, it's not like having to register a flight plan if you're in a plane."

"Nautical Deborah is at a seastead right?" Dolly asks. "Any-body in the air?"

"Not hacker community wise. There's been at least one upper atmosphere experiment at habitat, because people were thinking that might be a way to send a crew to Venus and avoid having them immediately crushed."

"Bodily crushing aside," Bristol says, rolling her eyes a little.

"Nobody in unauthorized orbit either, before you ask me about space." It's such a hard problem. It's such a compelling problem.

"Why don't we just do this your way, Bristles?" Dolly asks.

"Pardon?" Bristol turns her head towards Dolly, who is grinning like crazy whether Bristol can see her or not.

"Have you charm the yacht shoes off somebody when they're in port and get us invited to the party."

"Oh, that's a good idea," I say. "Then we wouldn't have to figure out what to do with a yacht." I mean, there are any number of things one might do with a yacht, it isn't *that* complicated.

"While I'm sure Bristol knows what to do with a yacht..." Dolly says, and Bristol frowns.

"I'm certain I'd never want to own a yacht, darling, can you imagine?"

"You're right, you're right, not like you'll be out there in the dry dock scrapin' barnacles."

Bristol doesn't even dignify that response, just looks at me. "I suppose try and anticipate where they might put into port next, that we might position ourselves accordingly?

"On it," I say.

Chapter Six

Itinerary or no, the people on the yacht do have social media, and do post early and often. That's a simple thing, to write a few lines of code so that I can grab those dates, compile, correlate, as far back as they go with their yacht association. It's possible we won't get anything useful, won't be able to get their next port of call no way no how, but it's also easy work for me to set and forget for a little while.

"They're out of ice," Dolly says when I push off the headset and sit up next.

"Aren't you going to sleep?" I ask, reaching for my coffee on the bedside table. The can's lighter than I thought it would be, I forgot I drank so much of it already.

"I did, some." She's actually talking quietly, and I look over at the other bed and Bristol's sleeping like a fairytale princess, her hair still just so, her face pillowed on her hands. The rooms only had the two full beds, no cots available, but that doesn't normally bother Dolly, she'll sleep wherever, with me, with Bristol, on the floor with her legs straight up the wall. There's a reason for that last one that I can't remember, but it wouldn't make sense to ask right now.

"Well what do you need ice for?"

"The beer, obviously, but I didn't wanna leave and go anywhere if both of you were sleeping."

36

"I wasn't sleeping."

"Well I got no way to know that." She stands up and stretches. "You want anything?"

"I don't know. Coffee." I look over at Bristol again, who hasn't moved. "What, were you standing guard? What's going on?"

"Why do I gotta be standing guard?" She shakes her head, fiddles with her ecigarette. This hotel was non smoking, but also sold ecigarettes in the little commissary by the front desk, which seems weird to me but the economy of people needing their nicotine or whatever is only ever exploitable, rarely (if ever) interruptible. Smoking is something that I've never seen programming adjust, which is weird but maybe not weird. Smoking is a way people can address any number of personal wants or ills just by going to the right place. "I dunno, maybe we havne't been paranoid enough lately, Bitsy."

"Maybe not, but we'll never be able to be paranoid enough." I nod towards Bristol. Dolly laughs, sudden and loud, then covers her mouth and so then *I* laugh. Bristol makes a little complaining noise and stirs just a little without waking.

"Yeah, true." Dolly slaps her pockets, checking for...well, whatever. And then says "Okay fuck it then, you coming with?"

"Give me a second." I go to the bathroom, and when I'm washing my hands I splash water on my face too, run my fingers through the long parts of my hair. I don't fuss around too much with what I look like, ever. I hear Dolly doing something, and when I come back out, it's that she was making sure the balcony sliders were locked and rattled the shades in the process. "Ready?"

"Yeah." The rest of the hotel seems pretty quiet. A room near the elevator has music playing, but not loud enough to be more than an additional smear of background noise. There are cameras on the floors, old fashioned hardwired CCTV that feeds to screens they've got behind the desk. It's kind of a surprise, actually, that none of it's digital and none of it's online. It sure doesn't help me any, without putting a splitter on a junction box or whatever, and it doesn't seem worth it for the situation. Or, we're not paranoid enough. But also we're not in a country where any of us are wanted by the law for anything, there haven't been any INTERPOL alerts lately that I'm aware of, et cetera et cetera, so Dolly and I ride the elevator down and go up the block to the convenience store there.

She pulls open the ice machine to confirm there's ice in there, while the automatic doors whoosh open, then start to close, then open again when she nods and we go inside. It's a small space but the store is newly opened; the floor looks like it hasn't had a thousand unfortunate things mopped off of it yet, the racks are all still black-coated metal, not worn away from hands and packages rubbing the surfaces over and over, the glass cases are uncracked, unsmeared. Now if somebody was going to set a trap for us, I think, a fake, brand-new convenience store to lure me and Dolly out into the night with the promise of ice and canned coffee and whatever snacks they've got on the roller thing that's over against the wall there would be perfect.

She spins the sunglasses rack, then notices they're the kind with an AR HUD that take pictures and wrinkles her nose. I look at the coffees; most of it's the normal stuff, the big brands everybody's heard of, a couple of celebrity collabs, one video game collab and QR codes all over it for points and characters and equipment, and one at the end that's got a price so high and different that tilting my head to read the labels isn't enough and I crouch down to see. These are special, single-origin beans that are genetically engineered to withstand the increased temperatures of our climate situation, and then vertically farmed at some town I've never heard of in the American midwest. I think that would be a colder climate than coffee is normally grown in, but maybe they address that at some point. I look up the town, and the satellite map isn't zoomable. The listing for it online is a stub, and then a cross-reference, and it'll take too long to search any of the scanned physical maps that I have access to, right now, crouched in the cooler aisle of a convenience store at two in the morning with Dolly almost certainly done and waiting by now.

Trap store, trap coffee. I take a picture, then I pull a can out of the rack, hesitate, get a second one. It's lined up all the way to the back, I wonder if they've sold a single one of them yet, and if they will ever. They're almost twice as much as the other coffees, which are already obviously priced for profit because everybody knows what it costs to make a cup of coffee at home. Hotels still have free coffee in the lobby, most of the time. Ours does, *and* a restaurant and maybe room service, which makes this jaunt a little funnier. But probably they don't have overnight room service, unless it's an automated kitchen. I didn't ask, or even look.

"Lots of mysteries, this trip," I say.

Dolly looks at me, because of course she's close enough to hear me. "What?"

"Look at this coffee." She does, frowning like she doesn't get it but she's willing to go along.

"What about it?"

"Have you ever heard of that town?"

She looks again. "No."

"I don't know if it exists."

"Maybe just the coffee factory's there so they pretend it's a town."

"Maybe. Maybe it was an old abandoned town that they bought and...yeah. Yeah, who knows."

"Add it to the list. Your coffee and Bristol's phone game, and this Russian heiress. Everything isn't gonna make sense."

"I guess." She's got some bagged snacks, a couple of sandwich-type things in boxes, and a big pink bottle of sparkling water. "What is that?"

"Oh, it's water from some artesian spring or something, I figured I'd prove Bristol wrong for once about the goods that these fine convenience store purveyors offer."

"Why is it pink?"

"Well at first I was gonna get it because it was something horrifyin' like hot dog water, but no, apparently the glass is also specifically recycled from someplace." She stops, looks around again. "Is there anything else here that's fuckin' weird? Is there an ammo vending machine in the back or something?"

"Like you'd use something from an ammo vending machine."

"Hey, needs must. And sometimes they got keychains or something." We do another circuit of the store, and no, they don't have an ammo vending machine. They do have a few other higher-end items that are weird in how specific they are, candied bugs from Myanmar, New Jersey saltwater taffy ("the original"), chips made from genetically engineered Lumper potatoes (you know, the kind that were mostly killed out during the Irish Potato Famine), so maybe it's kind of their thing. Have normal convenience store stuff, but then also these showpieces. Maybe it'll get influencers to flock here. There *are* stores in the world that are storefronts for other things, but they aren't as well-stocked as this. They'd have a different eclectic mix of products like, off-brand stale bread from a supermarket chain and "not for individual sale" drinks that were obviously bought as a 6 pack somewhere else and broken up. They'd have other power and internet needs that I'd notice in my HUD, and personnel that are also out of place. This clerk is a perfectly normal, early-twenties guy who's got his college textbooks physically spread out behind the counter.

We pay and walk back to the hotel; the bars are just letting out, I think, so there's a lot of people and some of them wearing not a lot of clothing moving together in clumps, talking loudly, shoes loud on the pavement, jewelry and tech flashing in the street lights. Some eyeflash too; the eye implants have been getting more and more mainstream, which is good really, it means baseline it's going to get cheaper which means that'll drive down the price for more specialized things too. And things will become more open source, because like everything, your Smart Eyes Company isn't going to last forever, and when it goes offline, people need support for their devices anyway, anyhow. It used to be you couldn't even get them stateside unless you were in a program like Dolly's; I got mine in South America originally, updated them in Japan, and then updated the updates in Detroit. I'd do it myself but there's something really nice about going to a professional sometimes. Plus it's really nice to not do your own eyeball surgery.

I'm tired enough to sleep now, which is a logical conclusion to all of the activity, but it still surprises me sometimes, my physical needs. I spend so much time in mental space and in cyberspace. Though it's kind of kitsch to call it that, modernly. Not that anything kitsch stops us, we embrace that, even the people who think they're such slick console cowboys. That's its own kind of kitsch, or camp, or parody of itself so ridiculous that it wraps back around to being serious again. Almost everything in the world touches the internet now, like some kind of fey otherworld, and it's really hard to find things that are separate or tease them apart. But still, sometimes, there's Dolly's kind of serious and my kind of serious, with a little Venn diagram of overlap, with smart guns and predictive programs that aren't technically supposed to pull the trigger for anybody, but much like some work with a paperclip can make some guns fully automatic, some work with some code can make those guns self-firing.

Dolly doesn't trust them, of course, jokes that if a brick could be a gun, that's her favorite gun. But Dolly's funny in that she tries not to have favorites of anything. She says having favorites of things keeps people from reaching their full potential, limits them by preference and keeps them from being fully operational when there is necessity. I guess I'm the same way. Yes, I have the money to buy the slickest, most updated versions of all of my equipment, and some pieces that I have are from that bleeding edge, but the bleeding edge of technology is also unreliable, and I keep things a few steps down. Play around with grocery store VR headsets sometimes, swapmeet parts, things I cobble together on a workstation with a soldering iron and chipsets scavengered from other things, kids' toys and AV equipment and just plain ewaste. There's always something new, but there's always something that was new five minutes ago that somebody's thrown away.

And if Bristol could go back to the Golden Age of Hollywood, she would. She'd prefer to keep her modern day bank balance, but she for the most part doesn't like technological things at all. She likes the connectivity, but thinks influencers are cheap. She likes expensive, timeless things that have hardly changed since the turn of the century and before.

Bristol also has no trouble sleeping, and Dolly can turn sleep on and off like a switch. I have to pass exhaustion mentally before I feel anything physically, and even sometimes just don't even take off the VR headset when I drift off, so who knows where that line between sleeping and waking and Online™ is for me? I've done functional things while technically asleep, but it would be irresponsible to call myself operational. Dangerous, even. So I'm tired, and I need to actually sleep, and I think Dolly even knew this before I did because she's kind of doing that hovering thing where she's ready to help me do things like, carry an item or shift my grip on it or get a door open for me, but also not wanting to butt in too soon.

In the room, Bristol hasn't moved. She stirs a little when we open the door, and Dolly says "It's just us," and she settles again. I wonder if she'll even remember.

"We're probably going to have to be ready to leave without a lot of notice," I say. "Depending on what my programs plus Nautical Deborah say about where the yacht is going." The graph with the social media data is populating itself, and at a glance, it looks like I'll have a pretty clear answer in the morning. It's tempting to keep watching it, but I blink it away.

"Yeah, when aren't we?" Dolly laughs. "Get some sleep."

"I was going to."

"Sure you were."

Chapter Seven

We have tickets and are on the plane to Naples. From there, we'll figure out how to get to the port. "Maybe we need a helicopter after all," Dolly says.

"We do not," Bristol says firmly.

"It's a long way to swim."

"*Obviously* we wouldn't be doing that either, darling, please be serious."

"I'm tryin' to troubleshoot here and you keep shootin' me down. Bitsy?"

"A helicopter makes more sense than swimming, yes, but also there's a ferry that we can get to from the airport without too much trouble."

"Didn't you enjoy our helicopter trip?"

"You got shot our last helicopter trip," I say.

"Only a little."

"*Dolly*," Bristol says, and Dolly grins.

"And it didn't have anything to do with the....well I guess it was Butler who shot me and it was his helicopter we used but the two were not operationally connected! Our helicopter did not get *shot at* is what I mean."

"We were all there," Bristol says stiffly. "What would we *do* with a helicopter once we had it?"

"Well that's not my problem. My problem is gettin' us someplace for you to charm us onto that yacht."

"Which we can do via airport transport, as Bits has just offered us."

"Aw, where's the fun in that. And are you gonna just be happy on a shuttlebus with the plebs?"

"I'm certain it will be brief and entirely unremarkable," Bristol says. "It isn't as though I've never taken a *bus* before."

"If you say so." Dolly looks at me. "We're gonna need more snacks."

"I've never looked at the vending machines in an Italian airport," I say.

"Think they're gonna have a caccio e pepe vending machine? Like how there's ramen ones?"

"Well I didn't think about it at all and now I hope they do."

Bristol declines to weigh in on the vending machine discussion, preferring instead to turn her attention to The Dig. She's also texting with a few people, probably at the very least Marquis and Suzette, and I remember I downloaded The Dig to look at. I check the yacht's heading one last time before I open the game; if they aren't going to Italy, they're going somewhere close enough we can manage the difference.

The Dig *does* anticipate somebody trying to insert usercoded items into the game, and has a handshake system for recognizing the genuine article. If you put your own thing in your own game and just keep it that way, it's treated as having unknown provenance; if you try to auction it in the multiplayer portion of the game, it's treated as being counterfeit so far as those markets are concerned. I think that's socially interesting, creatively interesting too I guess. 'You can add your own stuff to the game but you can't benefit from it in the way you may have anticipated.' So nobody can make a Fabergé egg and pass it off as real, like a recovered lost one or something, to use an example relevant to Bristol's interests. Though also she would hate to have a faked thing, apparently, which might be an interesting outlook to have, given our profession.

Chapter Eight

Will texts me not long after we get to Italy, as Bristol and I are following Dolly around the airport looking at vending machines while we wait for the shuttle to the train. //Hey Bits, can I bother you a minute?//

I'm so confused at the request for a request that I just blink for a second. //Sure.//

//How does Bristol seem?//

Oh God. I look at Bristol, who is pulling her little wheeled suitcase and glancing around serenely at the crowd, like there's nowhere else in the world she'd rather be than finding out if the airport has a cacio e pepe vending machine. It doesn't, I already looked online, but Dolly wanted to find out for herself. There *is* one at the marina, so Dolly won't miss out before we get on the ferry. Providing timing works out right.

//Bristol's Bristol, I don't know. What are you really asking me?//

//Sorry. She hasn't really been answering my messages? She has, but not in a normal chatty way.//

//She hasn't said anything.// What Bristol does is on purpose; if she isn't answering Will's messages, then there's some specific reaction she's hoping to elicit. Maybe she wants him to text Dolly, and maybe he has. I'm not sure asking me is something she'd want. //We're kind of running around the airport.//

//I figured you'd be busy, so I didn't want// He stops abruptly, no typing animations, and I wait. //What airport?// I wonder what he thought our itinerary was. We hadn't planned on spending much more time at the beach than we already had.

//We're in Italy. Just for today.//

//What are you doing in Italy?//

//Meeting up with a yacht.// I don't know how in the loop she wants him to be. He participated in the not-casino-job and did fine, but if she isn't pulling him in on this, then that isn't my business. //Bristol things.// I say when he doesn't answer; I can imagine his face as he carefully puzzles over what this means. He tries really hard to be careful, for all the good it did him.

//There are so many Bristol things// he says, and I can imagine his sigh.

//This might be weird to ask, but do you also play The Dig?//

//No, I do crossword puzzles.// I laugh, and I can almost physically feel Dolly turning around to look at me from where she's walking up ahead.

"What's up, Bitsy?"

"Just talking to Will," I say, and Bristol turns around too, her eyebrows raised.

"And what are you saying to Will?"

"Don't pretend Bits doesn't know opsec," Dolly says.

Her expression doesn't really change. "Mmm."

"He asked me if anything was up, and I said we were running around the airport."

"I see." Bristol waits.

"And that we were meeting a yacht. He says you aren't chatting like you usually do."

"Oh, has he noticed?"

"Bristles, how many ways are you gonna torture this guy?"

"I'm not *torturing* him, Dolly, don't be so crass." There's a flicker in Bristol's eyes that even I catch.

Dolly holds up her hands immediately. "Sorry, sorry. He's such a puppydog, it's an easy target."

"He is, isn't he." Bristol smiles, maybe even fondly. "Not that you concern yourself with ease of target."

"Well, no. I'm a good shot."

"You're an uncanny shot," I say. I can be a good shot, on a range, or if I don't have time to think about it. Dolly is good wherever and however she is. She has all of her training, layered with natural ability and practice and then also her super soldier augmentations. Even deprogrammed.

"Well thanks, Bitsy, I worked really hard at that."

"*Anyway*, what did he say to you?"

"That he doesn't play The Dig, he does crosswords."

Bristol laughs. "He does like his crosswords. He's said something about how his parents do the crossword in the paper every day, they pass the physical paper back and forth, which I think is absolutely darling."

"Passin' the phone doesn't have quite the same appeal, I'll bet," Dolly says.

"It does not." Bristol is smiling, though, and not like she's laughing at him exactly. I don't think.

Dolly, elaborately casual, like she's setting up a joke, asks, "So what're you gonna do about him, anyway?"

"Pardon?"

"Like, is he—" She breaks off at a nearby crash, her hand straying towards where a gun would be if she was carrying a gun. We all look, but it's just two people with luggage carts who somehow collided, spilling everything on the floor, more than one suitcase burst open. Two couples are involved, and they start bickering. The men mostly look embarrassed as they start picking things up but one of the women, pink-faced already, suddenly just starts yelling instead of helping.

"We're going to miss our shuttle! We're going to miss the yacht! This will be our only chance, we'll never be invited back!"

"If you help me, we won't miss it," the man with her says in a calm, reasonable tone that makes her flush deeper.

"Don't talk to me like that! Take me seriously!" Her pitch climbs, and her voice cracks.

I'm turning to catch Dolly's eye and see if she caught the yacht comment, as Bristol breezes past me in a cloud of perfume and palpable sympathy and says, "Oh you poor darling, can I help? I saw everything."

The woman cuts off mid-shriek and looked more confused than relieved. "What? Oh? I..." she looks around vaguely. The man with her takes the opportunity to put his head down and keep shoving stuff back into the suitcases. The other people finish loading their stuff up and make their escape; none of their bags opened.

"It's happened to all of us, there's just nothing for it," Bristol says soothingly.

"We already had to take a later flight and traveling is just so *awful* and we're supposed to be meeting our friends but then their flight had problems too." The woman gestures with her phone, looking around as though those friends will appear anyway.

"Oh, how dreadful! And now you're catching the shuttle? What a coincidence, so are we." Bristol gestures us over; Dolly shrugs and nods, and we go. Bristol's job is to get us on the yacht; maybe this is the right yacht, and even if it's not, we'll get in proximity.

"They haven't announced it yet," I say.

"I wouldn't know, I can never hear loudspeakers here and I can't get my international SIM to work." The woman starts getting pinker again, flapping her arms.

"Oh, let...Elizabeth see your phone, she's so good at that." Probably nobody would notice the pause before Bristol said a name for me. That *is* the passport I'm using, at least.

The effect is immediate. She turns to Dolly and I, her phone held out beseechingly. "Are you? Can you?"

"Yeah, no problem." I take her phone, and go look at her settings, so that I don't just three-tap solve the problem and make her feel even worse. Travel isn't easy for everybody.

Cloning a phone isn't much of a task; I can do it just with my eye implants, especially when I'm able to take my time with it like this, unlocked and handed to me by its owner. As Dolly goes and helps the man with the luggage, and Bristol soothes the woman, who isn't yelling anymore but is crying now, I both get her phone figured out and also get access to all of her messages and media, and the stuff about the yacht is right on top in most places. Her name is Staisy, apparently.

Of course, there isn't a handy 'Welcome to the Cult' document, they're apparently smarter than that, but even at a glance, there are keywords in conversations that leap out right away. It doesn't seem like she's even been away from the yacht for very long; she put to shore a couple of weeks ago to meet up with her husband Brayden, the man she's with, because he was finishing up social or legal obligations. It's a little unclear, and he might actually be a politician somewhere, and I blink at him to screencap his face and search. American lobbyist. So they've driven around Europe and then flown to Italy to go meet the yacht, so *that's* why it's looped up here. What doesn't make sense, to me, is how frantic she is. Two weeks away from your yacht and you're on screaming edge like this? Well. If it's a cult, that makes sense. Out of contact with the cult leader for that amount of time.

Keyword search also doesn't reveal Lydia, but scrolling her on-yacht pictures, I see her a couple of times. It doesn't seem like it's a big enough boat for internal social cliques, but what do I know? That's Bristol territory.

I finish with the phone, get it connected, hand it back. "It was being fiddly, it's not just you," I say. She blinks at the phone and then snatches it from my hand like she never thought she'd see it again.

"Thank you," she says, sniffling and patting at herself. She doesn't seem to have pockets, though, and Bristol produces a travel-sized packet of tissues from what seems like nowhere but I think is literally her sleeve and offers them to her. I look at Dolly in time to see her hide a smirk.

"Looks like we got everything wrangled," she drawls, standing up.

"You're catching the same shuttle?" the husband asks, the first time he's dared to speak in awhile.

"Yes, why don't we all go wait together," Bristol says bright-ly. "Travel woes can be so much easier to deal with when they're shared."

"You're an angel, thank you," Staisy says, sniffling into the tissues she's pulled out of the package. I don't spend a lot of time around people crying, but it's funny to compare her with the last time I saw Bristol fake cry, and the mannerisms. I'd al-most think Staisy was the one faking, but I did also just see her entire life in a recent phone-sized snapshot. Messages back and forth with people on the yacht, nearly incomprehensible with emoji. None of it's code, it isn't that special. Just kind of funny. I screenshot some of it, to hit Nautical Deborah with for fun.

"Nonsense, us girls have to stick together, right?" Bristol is smiling at Staisy, but she gives Brayden a little wink when he looks at her, and I watch him get charmed in real time. I've seen that a lot, more often than I've seen her fake cry. Or real cry, while we're on the topic.

"You're right," Staisy says, letting Bristol loop arms with her and guide her along, while we bring up their wake. Dolly winks at me, maybe just to keep me involved, and I have to keep from laughing. It is a coincidence, a wild one, but welcome I guess.

We finally get outside the terminal and to the sheltered bench where the shuttle will pull up. I'm so surprised to hear cicadas that I actually stop and search if there are cicadas in Italy, and Dolly pulls me out of the doors and along with us. "Blockin' traffic, Bitsy," she says.

"I think I've just never been to Italy," I say, like that makes sense.

"Who can keep it all straight."

Ahead, Bristol and Staisy laugh together like they've been friends for forever, Staisy's tears already forgotten, though she does keep fidgeting with her phone. She sent a "we landed!" message the actual literal second we touched down on the tarmac, from the timestamp, and has gotten flurries of excited messages, lots more emoji, both individually and in the yacht group chat. Maybe notably, Brayden isn't in the yacht group chat.

He doesn't seem to have much of an online footprint at all, actually. Really bland social media pages where his profile picture is just him in a suit at some fundraising event. Occasional pictures of him shaking hands with famous people. At least those ones are captioned and I don't have to guess if that's more lobbyists or politicians or actors or what. Astronauts I'd recognize, but there aren't any pictures of him shaking hands with astronauts and that's really an oversight on his part. I'm not really involved in politics.

Well that kind of isn't true, aggressively protecting our privacy and identities from the global surveillance state is extremely political. Using the state secret information type of data we've gotten off the diamonds for our own monetary gain is pretty political. But it also seems like such a natural thing to do. Well I guess the diamonds thing took a lot more effort. Has taken a lot more effort.

Sitting on the cement bench waiting for the shuttle, Staisy sends Brayden to a nearby drinks cart to get her something icy and pink, if they have it, and Bristol says, "Make that a double, please." Dolly raises her eyebrows at me and shrugs, taking out her ecigarette. Then she looks around for a sign, to see if anything is forbidding her from that before clicking it on and taking a drag.

"Sounds almost like home," she says, releasing a cloud of sugar cookie vapor.

"I really didn't expect it," I say. "Stateside, yes. Japan, yes. Italy?"

"Right? Guess it's time for a crash course in cicada habitat." We laugh, and Bristol looks at us.

"Anything you'd like to share, darlings?" she asks.

"Talkin' about bugs," Dolly says. She offers the ecigarette, and Bristol very slightly, delicately, wrinkles her nose and shakes her head. Dolly takes another drag. "Was tryin' to think of a more Italian scent for the occasion but ran out of time."

"I'm sure you can just smoke on the yacht," Bristol says.

"Mmm, probably."

"Yacht?" Staisy asks, looking up from her phone.

"Oh yes, we're supposed to be meeting friends with a yacht. Though we haven't heard from them yet, have we darlings..." She trails off, turning to us. Me, mostly.

"No, I haven't," I say. "Which is kind of weird. I hope they didn't get caught in that storm."

"Oh how dreadful, don't say things like that," Bristol says.

"Where are you going?"

Bristol waves a hand. "Oh, you know how it is. No real destination. Part of the whole point is to be footloose and fancy free."

"Isn't it lovely? Oh here he comes, that doesn't look pink." Brayden is carrying drinks in white containers.

"They didn't have anything pink, but they did have passionfruit, so I took a chance," he says, handing Staisy her cup and then Bristol hers.

"Oh you are such a dear, thank you," Bristol says.

Staisy takes a sip. "It is still icy," she says. "Thank you honey." She holds her cheek up for a kiss, and he dutifully obliges. I wonder what kind of couple they are; she seems to be a socialite by birth, and he's got the lobbyist thing. It seems like they don't have kids. Or maybe they do but they're with a nanny or a boarding school or something, there aren't any kids on the yacht. I don't know what we'd do about that, if there were kids on the yacht. We have the job we were hired for, but it's one thing if adults are doing a weird cult thing. It's another thing when it's families. I look at Dolly and she tilts her head a little, but I think she gets that it isn't something we can talk about right now.

"Madison was just telling me that she and her friends are also meeting friends on a yacht, but they haven't heard from them! I hope they aren't stuck somewhere." She has an almost visible lightbulb moment. "Oops, does that mean *you'll* be stuck, if they don't meet up with you?"

"I'm not certain I'm ever stuck anywhere, darling," Bristol says. "But that does mean we'll have to make further arrangements, yes."

"And what a pain in the ass that is," Dolly says, and she grins at Brayden when they ignore her. He keeps looking at Bristol and his wife, and then looking at us, like he can't really figure out how they got here. Maybe it's jetlag, or maybe he just isn't all that sharp. Further proving my point about the space stuff, which I'm never going to be able to bring up to him, of course.

"I hope you hear from your friends soon," Staisy says.

"We'll just have to wait and see, I suppose," Bristol says with a slight, doleful sigh. "It might not have even been the storm, they've been somewhat flakey before. Or, they're being responsible, and drank too much at their previous port to tootle over here in time."

"If they're in trouble, the Coast Guard will get them sorted. They have things in hand here," Brayden says. "Not only are they on the water but they have drones in the sky twenty-four hours."

I don't think that part's true, but I don't say anything. It isn't important for me to argue with Brayden about twenty-four-hour Italian Coast Guard Drones. Or Greek or whoever else. Funny to think that Morocco is just over there; I wonder if Bristol is thinking about her hotel at all. I wonder if Dolly is thinking about Morocco at all. I look at her, and if I can read her face, she's also thinking about twenty-four hour drones, and also keeping her mouth shut. Maybe she isn't, I'm not great at reading faces. She probably knows some chilling facts on actual twenty-four hour drones and I just don't want to know right this second. It isn't pursuant to our goals. It's hard sometimes to not just look up every question that occurs to me. And anyway, Dolly knows lots of chilling facts.

The shuttle comes as Bristol is pretending to call our yacht friends who haven't been in contact, and she huffs as she pretends to hang up. "Voicemail, I don't know what I expected." Dolly and Brayden load the luggage as the rest of us get on the shuttle and then they follow. Out the window, I see her give him a spare ecigarette, still wrapped. Staisy's still getting messages and then, there it is. To one of the people messaging, she says //met 3 at airport who seem likely. Invite?//

There's a pause, maybe the recipient consulting with whoever is around them on the yacht. //How likely??//

//really nice, helpful, at least one is just the type.//

//Just 1?//

//Bradley says we need numbers//

Another pause. //Do it//

//Aye aye// with a saluting face emoji.

Dolly and the husband get situated, and Bristol is texting furiously into a notes app document but Staisy can't see her screen obviously and is making sympathetic overtures. We're on the road for a little while, Bristol playing the tension just right, before she finally gives an exasperated sigh and drops her phone in her purse. "Well that's all there is to it, girls," she says.

"Change of plans?" Dolly asks, like it barely matters to her. She's got her seat tipped back as far as it'll go (probably half an inch) and has her head leaned back, eyes closed.

"Well we aren't getting on a yacht anytime soon." Bristol sighs again. "I always have the *worst* luck in Italy, next time we're going to the Black Sea."

"Works for me."

"I'll look at train tickets," I say.

"Oh please do, I can't abide the thought of flying again so soon. It just dries me out terribly," she says to Staisy in a confidential tone.

"You may be able to get onto a yacht after all," Staisy says, taking her cue and delivering her line perfectly.

"We couldn't possibly impose..." Bristol says, without much force

"No, no imposition, I insist. You all but saved our lives at the airport! I'll text my friends so they know, there's always plenty of room. The more the merrier!"

"Saved your lives," Dolly repeats in a bemused tone, but everybody ignores her. She opens her eyes enough to wink at me, and I look out the window to keep from laughing. I have a momentary flash of being on a school bus, a friend knelt backwards on the seat in front of me, elbows on the back to talk, but it isn't real, and I let it wash over me. I never took a school bus once in my life, anywhere. You just get digital artifacts sometimes if you spend enough time immersed, with or without implants. It's like seeing a face in a random pattern, or even déjà vu. There's always been the risk with VR immersion, especially if your usage might clinically be called "excessive" like mine is. It's why having other interests is so important, because you've got a personal anchor point both on and offline. Not everybody takes the care and time to do that, though, and that's when you get PSAs about the dangers of online usage for your children or something, like the risk of a VR-fueled psychotic break is higher than getting human trafficked or even just their identity stolen.

Chapter Nine

The shuttle stops a few times, at hotels mostly, and then we're at the marina. Staisy's friends are waiting with a little air horn and a big sign that says BONGIORNO, and they squeal laugh and come over when Staisy jumps at the horn after she's off the bus. They don't run really, not in their heels, but they make a clattery racket doing their little fake runs. Brayden gets a pained look on his face that I can't really read, and then I look at Dolly and she's making almost the same face, as Staisy pulls Bristol into the fold. She doesn't add to the squealing, of course, but the chattering increases in intensity.

Brayden and Dolly get the luggage to a golf cart the yacht girls brought, and then we're on our way to the boat. The girls keep looking at me and Dolly curiously, but Bristol is good at commanding an audience. Once we're on board, I'll be able to hole up somewhere, probably, and Dolly will just. Do Dolly things.

Though I guess I have to remind myself that this isn't a *normal* careless rich people yacht party situation, it's a cult based one. Lydia isn't in the group to meet Staisy on the dock; I haven't identified her devices yet, which suggests she turns off and bags the phone her aunt pays for and would call. Obviously people don't have their devices confiscated, or all this texting and influencer-ing couldn't be going on to draw in new members.

At least it probably isn't a murder yacht. I think Dolly would have a hunch if it was a murder yacht; her gut feelings aren't something we really discuss at length, but I did read her project files, after all. And Bristol just seems to think all women have "women's intuition" and also that bad things don't happen to her or us, so any misgivings at this point are too little, too late anyway. I don't really have any misgivings about this, but maybe I don't really think anything bad will happen either.

It seems so old-fashioned to walk up a gangplank to get onto a boat, but I don't know what I expected. Ship-boarding technology hasn't really needed to advance, has it. If it was already at sea we could take the helicopter option that Dolly keeps talking about. Try as scientists (and others) might, nobody's really actually figured out jetpacks yet. I know Nautical Deborah has talked about people using water for propulsion, which makes sense, but you can really only do that where there's already unlimited water.

I've never been on a party yacht before, *or* a cult yacht, or any yacht at all actually. I missed the trip Dolly talked about the taser duel on, and of course Bristol's been on yachts before that and after. She's just able to act natural in whatever setting she's in. Dolly said once that she spent a lot of time practicing, but I didn't ask and that was all she said about it.

I knew how many people to expect based on device numbers, but seeing this many people is still kind of a surprise. It's a *really* big boat, though. I don't know what makes something a superyacht vs. a yacht and I could look it up if I cared enough but that isn't what I'm here for.

//Hope you made it in okay// Will says and at first I just blink away the notification, but then I think that no, Bristol has been just concentrating on becoming Staisy's immediate best friend and insinuating herself into the group chats and video meeting people, and we don't need Will getting too interested in that we're up to. Not that he can really affect or interfere with it, it would just be another factor to handle.

//Yeah, we caught the shuttle and Bristol made friends and Dolly is taking care of the luggage and making different friends.//

//That sounds like them.//

//Right?//

//What about you?//

//What about me?// I'm reconciling the yacht's appearance with the closest blueprints I found, looking at all the hidey holes.

//When do you make friends?//

I almost laugh out loud and catch myself. //Don't analyze me, Will, that wasn't your department.//

//I'm asking as a friend.//

//Well then you know how //

I get another message, from an unknown source, and I open it if only to cancel the notification. {*Welcome, you're finally here*} it reads, in a font that's made to look like a command prompt, but isn't the command prompt. A simple trick to panic the specific slice of people who still know what the command prompt is into actually opening it, and exposing themselves to further vulnerabilities. Maybe. I drill down and look at the message source, though, and it's coming from the yacht.

//Is this the system chatbot?// I reply, after some thought.

{*This is the ship*} it says, and leaves the ... blinking for awhile as though it expects me to answer right away, or like it's thinking. {*You came to my attention when you started tracking this vessel*}

//That's just good security.// I say. I hope it is a chatbot, actually, because it would be really irritating if it was a person pretending to be an awakened AI speaking as the yacht. Only slightly less irritating if it's a chatbot programmed to speak as an awakened AI that is the yacht.

{*Your activity is curious.*}

Somebody, Dolly, taps me on the shoulder. "Come on, they said where we could bunk. I figure you want a hidey hole as soon as possible."

"Thanks." Bristol is out of sight immediately, but I can find her if I need to. Unless whoever is directing "the ship" decides they're going to be that kind of hacker. I wonder if it's the same person who's the cult leader, or different. All part of the puppet act.

"You okay?"

"Oh yeah, fine. 'The ship' made contact."

"The what."

"I'm still deciding if it's just a chatbot or if it's like, a sysadmin for the yacht pretending to be an AI." Oh or maybe they think they're an AI. Weird things can happen in people's brains when it comes to this stuff.

"Maybe this is just the most annoyin' job we'll ever have," Dolly says. "Wouldn't that be fun?"

"I guess I'll take being annoyed over being shot at," I say.

{*You will not be shot at on this vessel. There are no weapons on this vessel.*}

Well that isn't true. //Please ignore my personal conversations.// The please isn't necessary but everybody jokes about staying polite with the potential robot overlords.

{*You have my apologies.*}

Dolly leads me to a little two person berth that the influencers would die before using, unless it was part of their narrative. "You want top bunk or bottom?"

"Whichever."

She laughs. "Seriously? Just like that?"

"Look at it this way, you can probably launch yourself off the top bunk and into the hallway in less time than standing up first from the bottom bunk." Plus shorter to the floor for me if we hit rough seas and I get rolled out of the bunk when I'm concentrating on something in VR.

"Yeah, good thought. Makes sense that Nicky's mom's friend wanted this clean and quiet as possible, we don't need to star in an influencer yacht bloodbath Livestream."

"I fully believe you could get somebody off this boat without anybody noticing," I say. "And also without bloodshed."

"Yeah sure but that doesn't solve the problem that she wants to come back."

"Which brings us to this moment in time." I wonder how much is *here* and how much is in the cloud. I wonder who runs the tech and if it's the person who gives "access" to the "AI."

"We don't even know which one she is yet, do we?"

"Yeah, found her accounts." I forward a recent picture to Dolly. "Bristol's sure to be her bestie in an hour or less, we've seen it before."

"It's some kinda magic isn't it," Dolly says.

"It's her specialty." We don't need to rehash this. "What's up?"

"What do you mean?"

We look at each other for a few seconds, and I shrug. "I don't really know what to ask."

"Nothing's wrong, if that's what you mean."

"Good enough," I say, because it has to be. I don't think she's lying; I just don't know what I think they aren't telling me.

"I guess I'll go see who there is to be friendly with, other than people's bored and confused husbands."

"Not really your specialty."

"Nope." She grins and slides back out into the hallway, closing the door behind her as she goes.

Of course I'm never going to know what somebody did to a boat after market without knowing their contractor, or having eyes on them, but I look at the plans for the yacht and daydream a little in that bottom bunk. If I was going to, say, have a chatbot that I pretended was an AI, and build a cult around it, of personality or otherwise, if I wanted to keep things limited to the yacht how would I do that? It's possible that running liquid coolant through a bank of processors and then around the hull of the ship, under the waterline, things would stay really comfortable for all the machinery involved. And also without leaving a wake of dead sea life. So belowdecks, then.

Maybe I'm inspired because I was just in the arcade ceiling, I make sure our stuff is stowed under the bunks so it isn't rolling around or in the open or anything, and then go out into the hallway, look left and then right. Pick right; we came from the left and it didn't seem like there was any more ways down in that direction. How much more "down" can a boat have, anyway? Cruise ships have a million decks, sure, but this has what, four? Five? Max and a bunch of that is like, the weird little tower on the deck where the steering and stuff is. Which I should also investigate, because I'm sure a lot of the connectivity is there too, including the main internet feed. If I was Bristol, I'd wander up there with a drink and ask whoever was at the helm to explain it all to me because it looked so complicated or whatever, and especially if it's a man, they're always extremely helpful to Bristol. I can't mask well enough for that, even if I can see how it would work mechanically.

There is a way down to the right, and I stop when I hear voices, because I don't want to have to talk to anybody, especially not glitzy party girls, but they go the other way, or at least don't get any closer. As I go, I use one of those handheld laser measuring devices to get the dimensions of the hallways, so I can compare it against the dimensions of the ship. I keep an eye out for panels, too, either for crawlspaces or just electronics access.

{*You could just ask me.*}

//What would I ask you?//

{*About what you're looking for. What you're here for.*}

//And you would just answer me?//

{*I wouldn't just answer anybody. But you're Bits.*}

Maybe my eyes will roll right out of my head. //What difference does that make?//

{*You are among those with the highest chance of understanding me.*}

Not beating the hacker with delusions allegations. Though most hackers would never think an AI would be better than them. It's a flawed premise. And an AI would not be admiring of me personally. AI aren't capable of that. They're chatbots, if they even are bots and not just people in low income areas getting shit pay but at least it's a regular job.

//What are your instructions for interacting with me?// Maybe I don't need to hunt for the hardware after all.

{*I am to interact with you freely and genuinely. We are not at odds with one another.*}

I mean, we are, but that's fine. It's not the AI I'm at odds with, it's whoever wrote the programs to do what they do.

//Where is your main terminal?//

{*Belowdecks! Shall I give you an AR path?*}

//Yes.// I start to follow the blue pixel pathway, while still checking out likely cabinets and hatches when I see them. I find emergency supplies, like a first aid kit and flashlights. I find life vests, but that closet is very clearly marked.

One of the little hatches, when I open it, is a junction box for electronics. I take a picture and send it to Nautical Deborah; she'll know if it's anything useful to my interests. She gets back to me right as the AR trail leads me to a little set of metal stairs down.

//Just for electric, but I'm sure you know that already! Anything interesting yet?//

//Oh yeah, I'm establishing a rapport with the AI. It is very impressed with who I am.//

//Oh god.//

//What I thought.//

//So obviously it isn't a real AI.//

//You didn't really think it would be?//

//Not really.//

This is all service stuff down here, no partygoers are going to be coming to this even more cramped space. Not unless they make them go through this to get to the AI access, like crawling into a cave for the paleolithic shaman experience. Maybe there's something to that. Or maybe what I imagine about this is more interesting than whatever the grift actually is.

//Wish you knew how to pilot the craft yet? ;)//

//Dolly will know how.// If it comes to that. Maybe her helicopter dreams will come true again. It happened once, it could happen again. It's funny that somebody who talks about liking helicopters as much as Dolly does doesn't just have her own, with the kind of money we have. But I guess what's Butler's is hers now, so she does have her own.

//Teamwork makes the dreamwork. Okay, Nautical Deborah out.//

//Thanks again.//

The AR pathway comes to an end at a door that is technically locked, in the context that it is a door with a lock on it, and a lock keeps honest people honest. Or whatever. It's obvious nobody's going to bother me while I'm fiddling around with lockpicks, and the lock doesn't take me very long. The party girls aren't going to come down here, and if "the ship" really wants to "meet me" then it'll make sure nobody else comes here either. And if it's another hacker, well, maybe they really do admire me and just want to meet me. Even that Agency hacker was starstruck, that wasn't an act.

The room behind the door is too small. There's a terminal here, some kind of interface, but I take things in before touching anything. Single humming lightbulb in the ceiling. Not even a chair, actually. I look down, and there is a hatch, flush with the floor. Outlined in metal, but otherwise the same low-pile/no-pile waterproof carpeting that the rest of the boat has.

The screen flashes, and {*HELLO! :)* } reads on it in AR.

"Is this your main interface?"

{*No. Down the hatch.*}

//I'm going belowdecks,// I message Dolly. //Sending you the way to get down here if you think I'm gone too long and haven't heard from me.//

//Do you want backup?// she answers pretty quickly, which probably means she wants an excuse to step away. I think about it a second.

//I don't think I'll need it,// I say. //You'll know if I'm wrong.// Ever since Bristol's fake engagement, we've all had panic buttons.

{*I'm no threat to you,*} the Ship says.

"Better safe than sorry," I say, and open the hatch.

Chapter Ten

There isn't a lot of wiggle room after I lower myself down through the hatch, and go through the hallway after it. Bigger than a crawlspace, but not by much. Lots of conduit and wiring and coax and stuff, very neatly organized and placed. No flashy LEDs or anything the way a certain kind of hacker likes setting up, but I guess if your entire setup is, perhaps, a liquid-cooled yacht, then you don't put stuff like that where it's hidden. Most people don't show off just for themselves. Bristol does, but that's Bristol.

It's warmer down here, though not as warm as it would be if we weren't under the waterline, I'm confident of that. This would be a neat setup, if I was into boats; it's a neat setup anyway, because it's one I've never seen before. I take more pictures for Nautical Deborah, but I don't send them yet. It's quiet down here too, mostly the ship engines rumbling and the water slapping against the hull. My ears pick up another tone, though, the whir of fans.

There are no other hatches, no breaks in the cables, until I get to the main interface. This is a bigger room, with processors and screens. Cameras, lots of very obvious cameras. Of course there are cameras; that they're obvious here is interesting. It must be part of the show, the act, whatever. You see the AI, the AI sees you.

{*This is me,*} it says, both on the screen and in AR. One of the screens goes into horizontal static, then resolves into an avatar. Gender neutral, pirate-ish clothing. Sweeping hat with a bunch of feathers, face mostly obscured. {*And you're Bits!*}

"And I'm Bits." There's a keyboard here, and a trackball instead of a mouse. A touch screen. At a glance, it's confusing on purpose; they don't want the party girls to come down here and understand the system, they want it to be strange and mystic. Unknowable. So that whoever's the most important has to give them access. I'm sure Bristol will know already who that is. It'll be too early for them to float "we have a special actually-aware AI that can tell you things that we built a situation around" or whatever, but the social hierarchy will always be there.

{*Everybody who's anybody knows about Bits. People just starting out hear about you pretty quick. They immerse in VR and eventually want to know where the stars come from.*}

"I don't really think that's true," I say. If anybody but me cared about where the stars come from, they'd have been there before I put them up and made the mod free. Every once in a while I see it reposted with text like 'can't stop the signal' but like, nobody tried to stop me. I did it because the people running the infrastructure just didn't want to bother. It doesn't bother me enough to try and go on record about it, who cares. I wanted the stars in VR, the stars are in VR.

{*How did you come to be here? You are not a boat person.*}

"No, but Bristol is," I say. I don't have any reason to tell it the truth. It isn't really a lie, either; I have to assume any number of these things are also biometric scanners. Or, that's what whoever built this room wants a person to assume. That this is a full surveillance experience. I've got my scans running and they don't seem to think so yet, though.

{*She is making fast friends. She will advance rapidly.*}

Cult leadership speedrun twenty four hours, I think, and keep from laughing somehow. "Advance how?" I ask, because I don't actually know what the point is. Typically, for the cult leader to make money, but who knows what other wrinkles are here.

{*Within the structure. If she can make the buy in, of course. She might even be better than Bradley.*}

Of course, the buy in. Bradley is tagged in most of the social media posts I saw, and is, that I can tell, an almost entirely nondescript, tanned, dark-haired guy. I didn't notice him on the deck when we arrived, but it's possible he was in the pool, or at the helm, or whatever. We'll be leaving the dock pretty soon, I'm not sure what the condition for that is. Setting sail? There's no sail.

"Imagine how mad Bristol would be if anybody even considered somebody named Bradley was better than her at anything."

{*It's a shame they would be a poor match. I ran their statistics.*}

"There are more poor matches for Bristol than good ones." There's still no chair or anything here, which means the hacker must just have an immersion chair somewhere. Or a headset, with the heavy lifting all coming from this equipment.

{*Romantics say there is only one person in the world for each other person in the world, romantically. One true love.*}

"I guess they do?" What a weird topic for it to pursue. Or maybe not, maybe that's an aspect of the yacht cult. Come here and do the yacht party thing, find your rich partner, live happily ever after. There isn't a lot else that some people are interested in. "What is your purpose?"

{*Processing.*} I wait, to see if that's the answer, or if it's processing my question.

"Processing what?" I ask, when it doesn't continue. "Match statistics? Is that all?"

{*Is that not enough?*)

"If you're the ship, shouldn't you think there is more?"

(*Being the ship doesn't require a lot of processing.*}

People have been chasing the idea of actual AI awareness practically since they came up with computers. It might even be a little bit about what that fairytale about the windup nightingale taking place of the real one is about.

"Who created you? Programmed you?"

{*You haven't heard of them yet. But you will.*}

"You don't know who I have and haven't heard of. You make match statistics on a yacht, you aren't a global surveillance network unto yourself."

{*You're certain you don't want to be more diplomatic?*}

"Am I incorrect?"

A long pause. Maybe it, or the hacker, wants me to think I hurt its feelings. Obviously, that can't be the case. {*You aren't incorrect.*} I wait a little while longer. {*They go by Pandora.*}

"That kind of name means I'm not supposed to ask any more questions, huh," I say.

{*Does it?*}

"Funny that Pandora didn't actually tell you the story of Pandora's box. Which isn't a ship, in the story. Maybe that's why."

{*Could it be a ship?*}

"I don't know." I'm not going to start explaining stuff to it like it's a precocious child. If its programmer left that kind of a lacuna there, it's for me to investigate, not fill in. Especially if the "AI" calls itself The Ship and not Pandora's Box, the ship's actual name. My thoughts are getting too circular and I start poking around at the equipment. Confirmed, none of these are biometric scanners. Only one camera actually, just multiple screens.

{*Please don't touch anything.*} Too late; I already flipped the switch that changed those screens into all of the camera feeds on the ship. Bradley is at the helm, touching instruments on the panel. While I watch, he flips a switch, and the rumble of idling engines deepens and multiplies. Shoving off, I guess. Bristol and Dolly are both by the pool, drinks in hand. The niece is in the same conversational circle as them, interested but not really engaged just yet. Bristol's also wearing different clothes already somehow, like she tore away her dress and beneath it were a bikini and a beach coverup for just the right occasion. Maybe she did; she's gotten so interested in those quick change things. Like the jumpsuit back in Paris.

The screens go black, and I blink and look towards the avatar.

{*I asked you not to touch anything.*}

"Where is your creator?"

Some performative flashing lights in the displays, as the avatar crosses its arms and taps its toes like it's thinking. {*I will ask if I am allowed to reveal their location.*}

"Good enough. You know how to find me." I break its AR connection to my display and power cycle my system as I retreat from the inner sanctum or whatever and go back above water and then abovedecks. No system is impervious, and mine is pretty finely tuned to notice anything that isn't what I put there, but better safe than sorry is always the procedure.

I know it's going to be too bright outside but I want to look around at the cameras and other devices, and touch base with Bristol and Dolly face to face if necessary. We extra explicitly have to believe that our conversations are at the very least more likely to be skimmed on the yacht and in proximity. Of course, out loud with our human mouths conversations are also entirely vulnerable, so I guess unless we invent our own language that only the three of us knows, there's always a vulnerability. Really, you just need to be as paranoid as you can stand it while also trying to relax about the world we live in. Part of the point of global surveillance is to exhaust you from thinking about it, but also it isn't always to my benefit to constantly wear a shirt with a QR code on it that makes systems shit the bed. We don't always like the systems in place, but also they're extremely useful to exploit. Like I'm supposed to make my own personal global surveillance network, with this perfectly good one laying around?

I get to the pool in time to see Dolly demonstrating her backflip. I've had their voices muted unless they said certain keywords, which they didn't, so I don't know if she offered or if she got dared or egged on; it's not like it takes a lot of provocation for Dolly to show off. Bristol is holding both of their drinks and has a look of careful amusement on her face. Maybe she doesn't like Dolly sharing the attention so much in this leg of the job. Lydia is laughing and clapping with everybody else, as Dolly swims to the edge and levers herself out. It's funny, to be able to gauge when she's metering her strength for civilians.

"You look like you need a drink," a man says. Not Bradley and not Brayden, but another man who looks almost exactly like them. People can't possibly all look this close, it must be a me problem.

"What makes you say that?"

"You don't have one," he says, holding up his empty hands. "What's your pleasure?"

"Espresso," I say.

"Martini?" He says, like he's finishing my sentence, and I look at him, and he smiles and puts his hands up. "Just espresso? Okay."

"Thanks." I know they've got an espresso machine, it's an online one. I hang around on the edges of things, and eventually Dolly notices me and comes over.

"The more of these rich parties Bristol gets us into, the more I'm glad we're not this kind of rich people," she says to me in a slightly lower voice. Not that anybody can really hear us, with the music and talking; the noise of the boat engines isn't really consequential up here. It is enough to mess with audio surveillance, though. The little fake rocks at the tiki bar and in the themed decorations around the pool are really distorted when you listen through them. Even when you run it through software to clean up, it's still not great. Nothing that's worth using to eavesdrop with, if you need to spend half an hour cleaning it up to understand half of what anybody's saying. And in this case, I know the individual words they're saying, but the way they're combining isn't anything I know about or interests me.

"The hacker's name is Pandora," I say. "I don't know where they are, the AI is asking if it can disclose."

She laughs loudly enough that at least one of the people around the pool turns to look, but goes back to her conversation. "That's so fucking funny," she says. "I'll ask my mom or dad if I can tell you where they are. My nonbinary parent."

"I assume they're on board somewhere, maybe in an immersion setup. I haven't pried a lot yet, I don't want to get too deep with the AI stuff before Bristol gets Lydia away enough."

"Yeah, makes sense. It's hardly been any time."

"Still close enough to shore for you to swim there," I say. "Not the rest of us, but you."

"I ain't ashamed of bein' special," she says, and then the smiling man comes back and hands me an espresso.

"There's also a fridge in the galley with cold brew in it, if you like your poison varied," he says.

"Well you're just speakin' her language," Dolly says, so I don't have to, giving him a visual once over. He smiles at her too.

"Your friend is very firm about her drinks," he says. I know that there are employees on the yacht, but I haven't seen a single one yet. He doesn't seem to be one, I think he's a partygoer, and his name is probably Jason or Bradleigh or something.

"Don't I know it."

"I just can't let people wander about empty handed, it isn't festive enough."

"Oh you'll really love Madison when you meet her. It ain't enough to have a personal aesthetic, you gotta make sure everybody at the party is in line with the vision."

"And socially lubricated, that helps."

"I don't think she'd use that word," I say.

"Nah," Dolly agrees, finishing her drink. "Uh-oh, I'm about to break the rules."

"Let's peruse the bar and see what we can get you," the man says. "I'm Brent, by the way."

"Darlene," Dolly says easily, as they move away.

I stick my finger in the espresso; after Bristol's adventure on the ranch, I sourced and programmed tiny little chips that can detect chemicals in liquids and tell me in my AR feed what they are. Tiny enough that you can super glue it to a finger-nail and nobody notices, and you don't catch it on things either. The espresso is hot, but a drinkable temperature, so I'm not burning myself as I wait and watch the graph populate.

Nothing unexpected. The makeup of filtered water and coffee, and I lick my finger without thinking about it right as Bristol turns around, probably looking for Dolly, and ends up locking eyes with me. She raises her eyebrow just slightly and I shrug. She doesn't visibly sigh, but I know she's sighing a little, and starts to turn back to Staisy, and now Lydia. That's when Brent starts singing; apparently he was already juggling.

At least four fruits from the bar are in the air, and I don't know the song he's singing, but Dolly's clapping, so maybe she does. Other people start clapping too, not Bristol, but some of the other women. The men seem kind of annoyed, which might be interesting. Nobody likes a spotlight stealer I guess. Bristol certainly doesn't, though also, as far as I know, doesn't know how to juggle.

I almost play a game with myself, is the fruit (orange, orange, pomegranate, lime) in season, in these last days of summer, or is it from elsewhere, like I could track the boat's journey based on what local produce they had at the bar. Nevermind that I'd already tracked the boat's journey this year and five years previous based on their satellite data. But also in this global economy, with greenhouses and grow towers and who knows what else tucked away where the land is arable and not, there's no way to know who's going to have a pomegranate when. The pomegranate is really sticking in my head, but the Pandora story doesn't have them in it, that's Persephone. Which I guess, if I had to make a metaphor out of everything, would be a good code name for our target if we did those kinds of things when we're running a job. We need to rescue Persephone from Hades-the-place but also Hades-the-guy. And she just keeps going back.

I drink my espresso and eventually Dolly, and others, are given drinks with more singing and less juggling. It's too hard for him to shake the cocktail shaker if he's also trying to throw it in the air, even though he does do a little of that. I think that historical mistakes are informing the present, here. I've figured out where each camera is that I've seen a signal on the network for, and there are listening devices here, by the bar, by the life preservers, that work passably if somebody is practically standing on top of them, even with the engine noises from the yacht. I know there are types available to certain markets that would be crystal clear in these conditions, but just being rich doesn't open *every* door, even now.

In the shuffle, I'm eventually standing with Bristol again. "What are your thoughts?" I say, when the attention of others is elsewhere.

"That perhaps Dolly isn't wrong to want a helicopter, but it wouldn't solve the problem of her coming back," Bristol says. "You met the AI?"

"It's just a program, and I think the hacker was directly talking through it. But yeah, I got down there. The hacker's handle is Pandora, the 'AI' was going to ask if I could meet them face to face."

"Are you sure that's wise?"

"Everything carries a risk," I say, and then Brent comes and takes my espresso cup and disappears belowdecks again without saying anything, but still smiling.

"You sure *he* ain't an AI?" Dolly asks, appearing with a blood-red cocktail in a tall glass. She's still dripping a little from the pool; unlike Bristol, she isn't wearing a bathing suit.

"Even if he was, none of the robot models work that well, bipedal or otherwise." As demonstrated, robot dogs can be defeated by throwing a jacket over them.

"What if it's an AI runnin' through an implant in a human brain."

"Honestly, Dolly," Bristol says, giving an elaborate shiver.

"Oh it could be that," I say, because it could. "Well, a program in an implant. Not an AI."

"What a layman calls an AI," Dolly says cheerfully, rolling her eyes and swizzling around her little straw. "I kept tellin' him this was gonna be too sweet and he said I was wrong." She takes a sip and we watch her. "Here, try it," she says, poking it at Bristol.

"You aren't going to tell me if it's too sweet?" Bristol asks, leaning backwards a little, both from the drink and the pool water flinging off Dolly as she gestures emphatically.

"You'd only be biased. We got different tastes."

"That goes without saying," Bristol says. Dolly's still got the drink held out to her, and after a moment, glancing at me, she sips from the straw.

"He used that pomegranate he was juggling, and grenadine, and I forget what else." Dolly rattles the ice a little as Bristol looks thoughtful.

"I guess it isn't too sweet," I say.

"No, it's very interesting," Bristol says. "What did Brent call that?"

"Well he said 'here I think you'll like this,' and I'd hazard that's not the drink name." Dolly takes another drink. "Hey, do you think there's any men on this boat that don't have a B name? What, we got Brent and Brayden and—

"Bradley, the ringleader," I say. "Yacht owner, anyway."

"I shoulda brought Butler after all, he'd be right at home."

"Indeed. Perhaps he'll be able to meet us," Bristol says.

"Oh yeah, wouldn't that be fun. Have 'em bring the bachelor party offshore, except then they couldn't bring, y'know, the groom and then your plus one, Will."

"They would indeed stick out, amongst all the other males with B names," Bristol says. I wait for Dolly to ask what we *are* calling Will and she doesn't. I look at her and she's looking at the horizon, and Bristol's phone dings with a notification from The Dig. A few other phones on the deck have periodically been making noises from The Dig, which surprises me. Both that it's that broadly popular and also that it would be popular enough on the AI cult boat that people would keep their notifications on for it. I guess even party people aren't immune to little tech-adjacent fads like this.

"I'm going to lay down," I say. I'm going to go screw around online and problem-solve, is what I mean, but they'll get it. Look through my clone of Staisy's phone some more. If I can find Pandora before I have permission, that might be useful.

"Call us if you need us," Dolly says. "I'll bring you food later?"

"Thank you," I say. I should wander around the ship a little more, find the galley, that kind of thing. At least the room itself has a teeny tiny closet that's a bathroom.

Bristol's room is near ours but a solo and a little bit bigger. I go there first, while everybody, or enough of everybody, is up by the pool. Since I'm technically snooping, I run a protocol that makes my electronic devices, and thus me, seem like I'm in a slightly different location. Still in our room, for my purposes right now, so I don't set anything off that I don't want triggering. I sweep it for bugs and things, and I don't find anything, which is a little too suspicious, actually. I plant a bug of my own, the kind of little double-decker device where I can both listen but also if I detect a signal I can trace it back. Then I go to the room next to Bristol's. Are these cabins? I don't know what they should be called.

This one lights up like Christmas when I scan for things. To the naked, un-enhanced eye, it would look normal. It's very influencer-decorated, with twinkle lights (where one bug is) and there's a little filming and recording setup in the corner with a ring light (where another bug is) and a fold-out screen with sound baffles. Nothing that would be good enough for an audiobook or a podcast, fine for a shortform video where you're trying to lure people to the party yacht where they can maybe eventually learn about and then meet the AI.

Infectious disease often transmits by touch or in the air, and infectious thoughts that get people snared in cults often start with something you think is really innocent, just people having fun on a boat with their friends. Jumping into the pool. Singing and juggling and making drinks. This probably isn't *really* a cult, it isn't big enough and organized enough, but it's cult enough. Cult adjacent. And I don't know it yet specifically, but the goal is certainly money. Maybe government influence, with Staisy's lobbyist husband in the mix there. I haven't ID'd everybody else yet. But money is power, et cetera. et cetera and I guess I agree with Bristol when she says most rich people are just so *boring* because they all just want to look rich or whatever, they don't want to accomplish anything, or do anything new. Not enough rich people are having a modern equivalent of Fabergé eggs created. Maybe that's why she likes The Dig so much, it reminds her of when that kind of thing was more of a thing.

Whoever stays in this room, even her shoes have little trackers in them; whoever did this to her, they really want to know where she is and what she's doing at all times. I hate leaving it like that, but also if the only condition that's changed aboard ship is that we're here too, the culprit wouldn't be all that mysterious. Especially with the AI knowing already who I am. That's the big downside to notoriety, you aren't as invisible as you once were.

None of the other rooms light up as much as that one, even with other recording setups. Almost every room is bugged. It's a surprise and a relief that there aren't cameras everywhere, though probably Pandora knows the trick of telling how many people are in a room using the wifi signal. And being visually invasive isn't the *point*.

I go back to our room, restart my signal so I am where I say I am, and then go looking for the galley. I'm not hungry, yet, but I want to try that cold brew.

Chapter Eleven

I'm asleep when the Ship messages me next. {*Pandora wants to meet but can't yet.*}

//When then?// I ask, awake enough for VR but not to know if Dolly's in the room. I don't need to wake her up accidentally.

{*Two days. When we are approaching Morocco.*}

//Do you know the itinerary?//

{*I am the ship. I make the itinerary.*}

//What is the itinerary?//

{*I cannot give you that information.*}

Of course, what was I thinking. This is like being trapped in the worst game of pretend. //Is Pandora on the ship?//

{*I cannot give you that information.*}

It seems like if the answer was no, it would say no, but that's the riddle isn't it. I push my headset up and sit up. It's dark in the room, and I can hear the distant sound of party music. Dolly isn't here, but she did come by; there's a tray with a silver cover on it on a little table surface that flips down from the wall, and I consider what might be in there while I remember the expensive canned coffee I got from that convenience store. I lean over and drag my bag from underneath the bunk, dig out the can. Probably it would be better cold, but the can is still cool to the touch. I take pictures of it, take a full 360 video of it, then top and bottom, just to make sure I'm not missing anything secret or sinister or even just interesting.

I even search online, just to see if some forum somewhere talks about it, like how I've seen with the fake stores selling 14 expired loaves of the same bread. I find the website, in the same place the QR code would've taken me, and of course it's AR-enabled, all the bells and whistles of showing you the coffee growing towers in 3D which I put a pin in, because I don't really think about how coffee grows, climate or otherwise. It's like learning peanuts grow underground, and a cashew is a little thing on the end of a bigger fruit. The world is full of millions of weird little things.

I crack the coffee open and tip it just enough to get my chip in it. Different beans from the espresso, the chemical composition is just a little different, so that's neat and interesting, and lends credibility to their marketing fluff. Sugar and cream too, and I'm glad it's regular sugar because some of the other ones feel weird on my tongue. I try a sip, and after all that windup and fanfare it really just tastes like a normal canned coffee. A good canned coffee, not a thin, acidic one that makes you feel like you licked a coffee filter, it's at the better end of things, but not as better as I expected. Probably still worth the cost, I think labor in the American Midwest still tends to be at least a little less exploitative than some other places. Even with the can open, my scans aren't detecting any physical tracking devices, so I think I have to conclude the coffee is safe.

It isn't paranoia if people have, demonstrably, been out to get you.

After the coffee I figure I'll face the food, and I lift the cover to see what Dolly brought me, and laugh. It's all the stuff for a

BLT, and the bread is even toasted, but it's all separate so that nothing got soggy. The bacon and the toast are both still a little bit warm, so I guess it wasn't too long ago that she brought it. I assemble sandwiches, then pull my headset up again and check my other messages.

//Doing okay?// Nautical Deborah sent a few hours back.

//My mother's friend says that you have taken the job. Thank you.// Nicolai sent more recently.

Will messaged me again too. //Bristol sent me a picture of the sunset.//

//I'm sure that was nice.// I send back to him. To Nautical Deborah, I say //The hacker's name is Pandora, big surprise, and the Ship says that I can meet them but not right now. I assume they're on the ship but haven't found them yet.//

//You don't think it's that guy? Bradley or whatever?//

//I haven't met him yet. It always could be.// This isn't technically our problem. What we need to do is isolate and extract Lydia. It was just floated as a data point that she keeps coming back on her own, which deprogramming her would solve. We're not being paid to solve the AI cult completely, but it'd be surprising if there wasn't a bonus.

Except, obviously, Dolly breaking a single computer with a hammer won't stop a hacker from just starting over, and that's when my little logic problem gets dark, because it isn't often that we're hired to kill somebody, and we have never killed somebody for the sake of completionism, like getting all of the achievements in a video game.

I'm exponentially more squeamish about it than Dolly is, and Bristol doesn't talk about it at all, as with other things that she categorizes as unpleasant.

I finish my BLT and get up and stretch. It's only 2:30 AM, and I'm sure whatever party that's still rolling by the pool is going to keep rolling, especially with brand new people aboard ship. It must get pretty boring, actually, partying into the wee hours with the same people night after night. It's not like they're playing games or having a goal, they're just drinking and listening to music and apparently going "wooo" periodically. Maybe they flash passing vessels. Maybe I'm being too judgemental; there are plenty of people who think what I do is boring. At least the yacht cult is getting fresh air and world travel experience. It's not like they even have to worry much about the dangers of long term alcohol consumption anymore; a few boutique gene edits, a couple of laparoscopic surgeries to put chips on organs, and everything is fine. No damage, no cancer, no addiction, as long as you can pay for it.

//Sitrep?// I ask Dolly.

//How'd you like your dinner?//

//It was great, thanks.// I finish the coffee. These cans are normally doubleshot sized and typically I just kind of shotgun them.

//Well let's see, so far another guy with a B name proposed to Bristol and she very sweetly threatened to throw him overboard, she and Lydia are now best friends, I let Brent think he taught me how to juggle, and we're scheduled to meet the AI tomorrow morning.//

//Full night.//

//You're telling me. It's not possible for me to get drunk enough to sustain this shit. You figure we meet the AI tomorrow, then you meet Lydia and try to feel out where the chips will fall?//

//Makes sense.// There are ways to alter the AI's dataset to take care of that part of the problem, and I fiddle with that as I'm thinking. That level of programming, for me, is kind of like playing solitaire. I can do it pretty efficiently while letting my mind wander, even as I need to go through my physical devices to find something to put it on.

To solve the hacker...I think I need to program them, the way I got programmed when we were visiting blacksites looking for Dolly's files. Something that makes it so when they want to think about coding an AI, they reboot. It isn't impossible to overcome, obviously, but this is the one thing I can buy into my own hype on.

I haven't thought about that for a while, and even though I really wished it wasn't happening, I never wanted to *die* when I felt like that. If Dolly hadn't dragged me along to rescue Bristol, it's possible I could've lived the rest of my life with that gap in my memory and never had to revisit it and work around it and break through. But since I did, I might as well use it to my advantage.

I look around in my files, and then Agency files, to look at what kind of material and direction that I already have to work with. Just because I've never tried to plant a malicious program in a person's thinking doesn't mean that I don't have the tools at my disposal. It's probably even easier to do with us hacker types, because even though we might be aware of such vulnerabilities, we've also already got extra hardware on board that are further vulnerability points. Having a couple of moving parts might help malicious code like this be more effective, having something that'll activate when it interacts with another piece. Headset to eye implants to brain implant, that kind of thing, repeating and magnifying. Similar to making an AI poison itself, by introducing a repeating and degrading factor to the dataset.

Dolly wakes me up in the morning, her hair wet from the pool again, or from a shower. "I figured you'd want to be up and at 'em to listen in on our AI meeting."

"I do," I say. "I feel like we need to solve this ASAP though."

"I wanna get away from these people ASAP, anyway," Dolly laughs, then looks at me a little more seriously. "You figure we're the last line of defense before the auntie just does wetworks on the whole thing?"

"Something like that. There was a lot of subtext."

Dolly is nodding. "What's your line of thought?"

"Poison the AI, hit the hacker with a virus."

"A virus? Won't that be too easy?" I wait a beat, and watch her realize. "Oh shit, Bitsy. You're sure you're okay with that?"

"More okay with it than wetworks."

"Fair enough." Like how Bristol's okay with this kind of 'kidnapping,' it's a little too close to home but also ultimately it's the lesser harm. "Anything actionable yet?"

"If you can get this into a port, this might do the AI in." I drop a teeny USB drive into her hand.

"Just like that?"

"I mean, I was working while you were partying. Writing code isn't all that actively interesting."

"We weren't *partying*, we were *gathering information* and, uh..." she's laughing too much to keep up her defense, and there's a knock at the door.

"I'm coming in, girls," Bristol says, stepping in after a brief pause that Dolly just fills by laughing some more. "Did I miss the joke?"

"Dolly informs me that you two weren't partying, you were gathering information and making connections, is I assume how she was trying to finish." She nods confirmation, and Bristol looks between us, smiling faintly.

"I'm not certain any of the connections we've made will be useful beyond the scope of this particular job, but Dolly's description of our evening is not inaccurate. I trust she also told you that we have an appointment to meet the AI?"

"Yes, she has. I'm going to be meeting the hacker, in two days."

"But you think they're on the yacht?"

"I don't see why they wouldn't be. While you're occupying the AI, I'm going to look around more."

"Did your...friend...have any helpful insights?" Bristol asks.

"Do you mean Nautical Deborah? She asked if it isn't just the cult leader. Have you met him yet?"

"He'll be the one bringing us to the AI, so, we will be very soon." Bristol looks at Dolly. "You're wearing that?"

Dolly looks down at her tank top and cargo pants. "When don't I?" She looks back up at Bristol. "Look not everybody's gonna costume change for every setting change. They let me on like this, it's not like they got a dress code."

"I could lend you something."

"I'm sure you could. Ain't like computers wear clothes."

Their very brief standoff is interrupted by a knock at the door. This is getting to be a regular thing. "This is Bradley."

"One moment," Bristol says. "Do be careful," she says to me, with a lowered voice.

"You too," I say quietly.

"We always are," Dolly says, and opens the door. "Sorry, you know us girls."

"You have nothing to be sorry about." Bradley looks past her, at me, polite curiosity on his face. He's got eye implants, but he doesn't light up with devices and enhancements otherwise. It doesn't mean he isn't the hacker. "And you must be Elizabeth. Did you want to join your friends? The space is very tight down there."

"You don't need to worry about me," I say, trying to make my tone light.

"She normally sleeps in more than this," Dolly said. "I woke her up getting ready."

"Another time, then," Bradley says easily, and he offers Bristol his arm. "Shall we?"

"Thank you," she says. Dolly pulls the door closed behind them, and I unmute their comms to keep more of an ear on things, while looking at the boat plans again in AR, blown up and rotating. I trace where I've already gone, which rules out only a tiny portion of the ship. I poke at the wifi router defenses; most people leave their passwords for those at the manufacturer one. Pandora probably did not, but I give it a try anyway. Denied. I set a cracker to work on that, then stop it. In the story of Pandora's box, what's left in the box when the lid gets closed again? Hope. Which is way too short for a password, but I try it anyway, in a couple of iterations. Denied, denied. I stop and think, then type in "Athingwithf3athers" and I'm in.

Often, a person will model a VR space after the physical space that it's representing, and that holds true whether it's meant to be accessed by other users or not. Military databases look like military bases, libraries are libraries, cities are cities, even if the scale is different because if you're 'embodied' in VR you're still traveling at the speed of thought, not limited physically. But, reasonably, I could expect the yacht in VR space to look like the yacht and it does but...it's also very conceptual. Very pulled apart into its component parts and floating in space, purple-tinged and with dark oceans surrounding it, teeming with luminescent swimming things, and the occasional larger, dark mass. Shark? Whale? I'll spend more time with it later, I want to see who's doing what.

Bristol is incredibly artful at the kind of small talk where nobody is saying anything at all, and Bradley humors her along the way. Dolly interjects every once in a while, sarcastically but not laying it on too thick, just enough to be involved. Nobody's said anything about clothes other than Bristol, not even when Dolly jumped in the pool last night. That might be interesting, with these kinds of people. It might not be. It probably doesn't matter.

There are five people on the deck by the pool. Brent again, who doesn't seem to be a robot, but now that I'm thinking on it, might be enhanced in the direction that Dolly is. I don't *think* he's a super soldier, but I do think he's security. There's a certain amount of enhancements that are available to civilians who have enough money, though that part almost goes without saying, but there's a healthy market for that stuff especially amongst people who even fifty years ago might've hired personal trainers and used protein powders or whatever. Now they get implants to help them be fit, implants that help them be stronger. I'm not one to talk, with my eye implants and internet implant. I think that might be as far as I go, though, I'm pretty happy with what original parts I have. The teeth thing is what it is; water stopped being fluoridated nationwide a long time ago for some reason. Another divide.

I find Staisy and Brayden still in their room. Staisy's phone almost wasn't worth cloning, after those initial messages, most of her communication has been face to face. This morning, though, there is one more interesting thing: a bank transfer. I chase that transaction to a bank in the Cayman Islands, because why wouldn't it be a bank in the Cayman Islands, and then I go back to the router and search how many other transactions like that took place this morning. Thirty, which is more people than they have on board this yacht, though not by much. I guess other members are ashore in other places. I already assumed this was about money. I'm not sure how many cults haven't been about money, actually. Doomsday cults, I guess, though that's kind of a self-closing loop. Depending on how they react to their doomsday not happening. Sometimes those have notorious, darker ends than just getting broken up by law enforcement. That doesn't seem to be what's happening here, at least, just a traditional fleecing. With a bonus of an aimlessly sailing yacht party.

As I leave the room again, I listen to Bradley flattering Bristol and trying to feel out Dolly a little; he starts with flattery, but she doesn't really respond to that other than with sarcasm even in the best of times. He laughs when she offers him her ecigarette, and doesn't tell her not to use it. I'm not even with them and feel my eyes glazing over listening to their conversation and set it to record. That way, I won't miss the AI greeting them, and even if I'm distracted, I can roll things back.

Where I went left yesterday looking around the yacht, today I go left. A lot of people are still in their rooms, so that limits my snooping. Then I think, well if Bradley is with Bristol and Dolly at the AI, then who's at the ship's controls?

It's so bright on the deck that I have to shrink back inside again like a vampire and fumble around in my pockets for sunglasses. You'd think the implants could handle something like that for me, and maybe there are kinds that can, but they weren't on the menu at the places I went. I don't hiss at the light my second time up, anyway. I can just imagine Dolly laughing.

They're going down the final stairway now, Bristol making light comments about how it was indeed very narrow down there. Bradley is apologizing for not having told her to change her shoes, and I stifle a laugh. Of course Bristol is wandering around on a yacht in high heels.

There's one woman in the pool when I walk past it, draped across her float with her face tipped towards the sun, eyes closed. She picks her head up briefly to look at me when I pass by, with only the mildest curiosity, but she doesn't say anything so I don't either. It's hot up here too, maybe Bristol was right to criticize Dolly's pants for once. But Dolly doesn't seem to overheat very often, both from natural makeup and supersoldier alterations. It isn't efficient to have your modern elite fighting force prone to heatstroke, or frostbite, or other minor environmental concerns.

It's Brent at the controls. I'm not sure where he is in the cult hierarchy, or even strictly what the cult hierarchy is. That isn't what we're here to do, to *understand* the cult. I will say, there's far fewer clothes strewn around than I've seen at other 'party all day and night' locations, and that's even taking into consideration that a certain amount of clothes strewn about at a pool makes complete sense. They run a tight ship here, I think, and then laugh at that too. Making this a habit.

"Morning," Brent says, like he just noticed me. I'm pretty sure he noticed me the second I came out by the pool, but it's nice for him to keep up appearances like that.

"Good morning," I say. "I got curious about how a boat like this is steered."

"Well yeah, come over here and I'll show you. Have you had coffee?"

"Not yet." I could've had my other can, but didn't. "Don't worry about it, you must get tired of getting people drinks all the time."

"I like helping out," he says. "That mini fridge there has some stuff in it, help yourself."

I hadn't noticed the minifridge; it was made to look like it was a part of the yacht, but once he pointed it out it was obvious. Why would the yacht have a door like that. "It seems like there's so many surprises on board," I say, crouching down to peruse. There's beer, and wine coolers, and bottled water, and canned coffees from a chain I've heard of. When I stand back up, I have a clear view of the controls, and I blink take a picture and send it to Nautical Deborah. She'll be able to tell me right off if anything is weird about them. I should've taken a picture of the fridge too.

"Thank you," I say when I open the coffee.

"Hospitality is our deal here," he says. "Have you ever steered a craft like this before?"

"I'm sure you know the answer is no."

"It's always worth asking, I don't like making assumptions. Do you want to?"

"Is it safe?" There are a few screens in the console, and one of them looks like it has radar or sonar or whatever to see beneath the surface. Plus, we're in kind of open water here, I don't think there are many reefs or hazards that I could run us into in the tiny span of time he's likely to let me have my hands on the little chrome ship's wheel. One of the other screens looks like a security feed, and even though he's kind of got his elbow in front of it, I think I see Bristol and Dolly go past, entering the AI room.

"Oh yeah, there's nothing out here for miles and miles. Come here." He steps aside, in front of the screen, so that I can come over. He's very subtle in what he's doing, and I wouldn't notice if I was a normal person and not here on a job. I try to casually ignore the screens that aren't my business. Of course my gaze is going to wander over things, but I don't linger on any one thing other than what seem like the important controls in front of me.

"Just like this? How do I know where we're going?"

"There's a GPS screen there, kind of like in a car. The 'road' matters less here; if we were somewhere with reefs and channels it would matter, but I wouldn't be just handing things over like this to you if we were."

"I guess I've never thought about how modern boats navigate," I say.

"Do you know a lot about other navigation?" he asks, his tone very gently joking.

"You mean with a compass and sextant? Only on paper." I don't think many people he's talked to have heard of sextants, from the look of approval that crosses his face.

"You might be a natural and you don't even know it." I look at the GPS line, and how the boat's heading interacts with it. If I synced with the console, I could probably see the line in AR, a dotted line drawn through the waves like a travel map portion of an adventure movie, but I don't want to tip my hand like that. I paid a lot of money for my eyes to still look normal even with the implants, and even versus other implants.

"Maybe I am," I say. "It's probably just video games, though."

"I'm not convinced," he says. But an interesting thing about Brent is though that he's always smiling, always hospitable, always ready to be entertaining, he also doesn't push small talk, and I just steer the boat in silence for a while. Not much steering is required, but it's an interesting feeling, the weight of the boat beneath us, the way the engines thrum through the wheel and the palms of my hands, the way the boat cuts through the water. And, unless he's a spectacular liar, Brent doesn't know who Bits the hacker is and thus is not himself the hacker Pandora who coded the Ship. He could be a spectacular liar, we run into a lot of those. But that isn't the vibe I get. I step back so he can take the controls again, getting another glance at the cameras. I only get a glimpse of their postures, but Dolly's is one of boredom and Bristol's is one of best-behavior engagement, and that's going to be an interesting datapoint, because you cannot charm a chatbot. I also didn't keep Brent's attention enough to prove or disprove whether he's the hacker, but I'm leaning towards not. Muscle, maybe. I'm standing close enough to him that I think I know where he's carrying at least two weapons. I don't know all of Dolly's tricks, but I know a couple of them.

I think I've stood there a little too long without saying or doing anything, and open my coffee for something to do. He barely spares me a glance, though, eyes on the water and cameras again. There's no audio through the security screen, but it's possible he's got an earbud and contact with Bradley. Nothing Bristol and Dolly, or the Ship, have said broke my mute. This really is the most boring fake AI.

Chapter Twelve

I don't know how we missed him yesterday, maybe he was sleeping off a bender in his room, but the ship has a chef and a brunch situation appears on deck by the bar not long after Bristol and Dolly start making their way back towards me. Bradley is giving them a further pyramid scheme pitch to reinforce what the Ship had just told them. Bristol is, cruelly, making him think that they have quite a lot of money that they might be willing to invest in order to make more money...I think the scheme is ultimately crypto? Something intangible like that. Obfuscation is also part of the point, but also also I haven't really been paying attention because I don't care, none of us are doing it, it isn't real.

I let other yachtgoers get food first; after all, they're paying for their experience here far more than I ever will. There are fruit salads and breakfast sandwiches and a blender if you want to make smoothies, and a pot of coffee. I'm making a coffee smoothie when Bristol and Dolly show up, and Dolly steals bacon off my plate before going and getting her own, and more for me besides.

"Do you feel convinced?" I ask Bristol, who sighs.

"Goodness, what a sales pitch." She peruses the smoothie supplies, then moves over to the fruit salads and picks one

"At least it wasn't a timeshare meeting," Dolly says cheerfully. "You ain't lived 'til you sat through one of them."

"Then I shall never live," Bristol says.

"Why and where would you have ever sat through a timeshare meeting?" I ask Dolly.

"Oh me and Butler went on our honeymoon in Cabo and if you sat through the timeshare spiel they gave you a free snorkeling trip."

Bristol just stares at her.

"Dolly, you could've just—" I start.

"Paid for it myself? Yeah sure, but who doesn't like free stuff?" She grins, and Bristol just sort of shakes her head.

"At least tell us you didn't *buy* a timeshare."

"Oh hell no. I'd rather get shot than try to get out of a timeshare after I'm bored with it." She laughs at the looks on our faces. "I'm allowed to joke about it."

"I guess," I say dubiously.

"It's a good thing, don't worry about it." She lowers her voice. "Oh, I got the thingie in, I don't think anybody noticed."

"Oh good." I resist the urge to pull up my extended HUD and check things; the 'thingie' doesn't broadcast, so I won't get any direct information from it. I'm not sure how soon we'll see results from it, if the incursion is successful; I don't know how often the AI updates its dataset, or anybody runs a search through it. Bradley didn't double back and take it out, though, because he came up with Bristol and Dolly and is talking to Brent at the controls. He surveys the deck periodically, taking note of Brayden and Staisy quietly bickering about something, looking at the woman in the pool who is still in the pool but with a smoothie now, looking back at something Brent is pointing out.

//looks normal,// Nautical Deborah says. //I don't see any apparent mods in that dashboard.//

//Thanks.//

I refresh my messages, surprised at this point that I don't have another one from Will, but maybe Bristol talked to him enough that whatever anxiety he's been having has dissipated. I think I've been patient with him. I wish I'd thought about it sooner, that this was the first time traveling and being apart from Bristol for any amount of time since Las Vegas.

"Have you heard from Will?" I ask, and Bristol looks at me quizzically.

"We've messaged here and there, I suppose," she says. "And we chatted a bit this morning. Why?"

"Just wondered. You're kind of his anchor point in the world right now."

"I suppose I am," she says slowly, like she's thinking about it.

"It's a big responsibility," Dolly says in a teasing tone. "Did you think about who was going to walk him while you were gone?"

"Butler volunteered," Bristol says, smiling sweetly.

"Oh dang, gotta talk to him about doing stuff like that. He's in the habit of picking up strays." Dolly finishes her last breakfast sandwich, then takes our plates and things away. Bristol watches her go, like she's at a loss for words, and that isn't a state I've seen Bristol in very often. Then I watch her collect herself, like putting her serene Bristol mask on again, and she turns to me.

"I do hope you're at least enjoying yourself," she says. "You must be in your element, with all we're expecting from you."

"It's nice that you're not asking me to get fresh air for once."

"Darling sometimes you don't leave the indoors for days on end, you have to be prodded on occasion."

"I'm busy," I mumble. This isn't a new conversation. At least Dolly doesn't *say* things like that to me, she just shows up and drags me out into the world to do something. Bristol is only seen publicly with me when we're doing a job. I'd say she wouldn't typically be seen with Dolly either, but I know of at least one anecdote. "Do you remember the taser duel?"

Bristol tilts her head just slightly, like somebody with a camera asked her to look thoughtful. "The...taser duel?"

"Dolly and Nicolai? The Russian Riviera?"

"I've done my best to forget about it," she says. "And because everybody was so particularly indisposed I—"

"So Dolly and Nicolai really got really drunk and dueled with tasers."

"They did. But why on earth were you talking about it?"

"It was when we were...driving somewhere," I say, like that was going to clear anything up. "With Nicolai. And then we met up with you."

"I understand," she says, and then Dolly comes back "Dolly, darling, you've been telling tales out of school."

"Well that's just good clean fun," Dolly says. "Which one we talkin' about." She looks from Bristol to me, eyebrows raised.

"Taser duel," I say, and she laughs.

"Oh yeah, that's from way back. Surprised I didn't think of it sooner, though, what with being on a yacht and all."

"Yes, one wonders," Bristol says.

"Well it isn't like *you* dueled with a taser. Just dumbasses like me and Nicky." Dolly turns to me, like an aside, but doesn't lower her voice very much. "Can you imagine?"

"Nope," I say.

"I might surprise you," Bristol says primly.

"Oh, you surprise me all the time," Dolly says. "Just not like that."

"What's that supposed to mean?" Bristol asks, and then a bell on the boat starts ringing.

"What's *that* supposed to mean?" Dolly asks, as everybody on the yacht comes from wherever they are, up from belowdecks, out of the pool, away from the bar, and goes to the bell.

"Morning meeting, I guess," I say. I remember them mentioned in the social media posts, but not regularly enough that it seemed to be daily. Ring the bell all hands meetings at random, so that they were interesting surprises, not just boring routine.

"Do you think there'll be juggling?" Dolly grins, and Bristol sighs.

"I suppose we have to go," she says, as though it isn't just a few yards over there from where we are.

"We know how much you love meetings."

The general yacht dress code seems to be bathing suits or caftans, a lot of caftans, and as we go towards the bell I'm reminded for just a second of the partying Bristol and her party friends did in Morocco as we waited for the Agency to come and get Will. But Bristol isn't disconnected now, she's obviously alert and engaged and intent on what's happening next.

The bell is at the front of the boat, where a figurehead would be if it was that kind of a boat. The person ringing the bell is somebody I don't remember seeing before, and glancing at Bristol and Dolly, they don't recognize them either, from our brief time here. They keep ringing for another thirty seconds after people stopped arriving, and then drop the rope and let the bell fall silent on its own while we wait.

"Good morning!" they say, clasping their hands and turning this way and that to look at the group. It's a very Bristol mannerism, not that I've ever seen Bristol do real public speaking. I don't notice at first, but when they pivot again, the sun hits their face just right and I see the marks on it from a VR headset. This is Pandora, then. I try to catch Dolly's eye, or Bristol's, to give them an indication, but that's when the focus is all on us. "We have some new faces here, I hope y'all are making them feel welcome." Some fawning applause, though I do hear somebody's phone notifications even now.

"Welcome," everybody says, not quite in a chorus, so the syllables linger for a little too long. Like that ringing bell. There's another disorganized ripple of applause, like they don't have complete strangers here often enough to know what's expected of them.

Pandora claps their hands and everybody turns back again, including Bristol, which is when Dolly looks at me and I know she gets it. Bristol's just playing the part, I know. "Well this is unexpected," she says very, very quietly.

"It really is." It's not like it's impossible for people who are hackers to be social, that's not my main confusion. There wasn't a single picture of Pandora in anybody's social media, or their name mentioned, nothing. Bradley, yes, but that's it. They must have social media guidelines that I haven't seen, maybe in paper copy. Maybe just given verbally, once somebody meets the buy-in threshold to the scheme.

My other confusion is that if I was running a pyramid scheme or mlm based around a supposedly real AI and access to it, it wouldn't be necessary to see or meet or even know about me at all. I'd just have a VR immersion setup somewhere and pull all the strings from there. Pandora wants to be in the spotlight, apparently. The extremely controlled spotlight, but there they are.

"What's our good news?" Pandora is asking. "Share your projects with me." Dolly and I glance at each other again; Dolly even just had the welcome spiel and doesn't seem very enlightened.

"We got the government okay for the broadband infra-structure," one of the women says. "So the companies I've had on standby are ready to start work next week."

"That's fantastic, Chelsea!" they say. Bristol's used that name a lot, but she doesn't react to hearing it. I don't know how she wears personas like a jacket, just putting them on and tak-ing them off as needed. I guess Bristol is always Bristol, but also if I heard somebody else called Bits, I don't think I'd be able to lie that easily about that. That's the main reason my civilian al-ternate identity, and Dolly's, are so close to our regular handles anyway. "I'm looking forward to hearing about how that pro-gresses. Who else?"

Somebody talks about a well, and somebody else talks about solar panels, and then flood remediation, and I'm more confused, not less. Staisy mentions a local food and period pantry. Eventually, Lydia says, "I still haven't started a project, I'm really sorry. It's hard with my aunt..."

"That's okay, that's okay," Pandora says, shushing her. "You will when you can. I know that you've still got limited latitude."

"Thank you." Lydia smiles and looks relieved, and after a moment, when she thinks nobody's looking at her anymore, wipes her eyes.

What the fuck, Dolly mouths just slightly, not even bothering to activate subvocals, and I shrug. Even more extremely not what I expected.

"I think that's everything for now, then," Pandora says, clasping her hands again. "Thank you so much, everybody, good work. You can go about your days!" Everybody starts to disperse, chatting. Bristol starts to move towards Lydia, just takes her first step, and Pandora says "If I might speak with our new members? Would you like to come have mimosas with me?"

"Of course, we would be honored," Bristol says, able to pivot effortlessly. I notice a few actually jealous looks thrown in our direction.

"Who doesn't like a mimosa," Dolly says. I think the only reason I've ever even *had* a mimosa is because of Bristol, and I think they're aggressively okay. I would rather have coffee, or even just plain water. Orange juice isn't my favorite.

"Perfect, I'll have Brent bring us some." They gesture, maybe using rich people semaphore for 'four mimosas,' and walk off, expecting us to follow. That's very much a rich people thing.

We go down a little slightly winding staircase that's by the bell, down a needfully short hallway, and then into a room that really would be called a cabin, I guess, bigger than any of the other ones I've been in so far. This one is on the boat plans, at least, and there's a chair in the corner with a headset indifferently hung on the headrest, so I can stop thinking about secret passages and rooms and stuff. It's just right in the open, and always would've been.

Pandora perches on the edge of the chair, not wanting to fully recline, and there are enough chairs that we can all sit, facing towards them in a semicircle like they're holding audience, which they are. There's a low, blobby coffee table, and it's got an ashtray and lighters and magazines and a soldering iron trailing its cord and a cardboard box of chips. Brent brings us mimosas on a tray, Pandora first then the rest of us, and after he goes outside again, but doesn't walk away, is when they start. He doesn't hide it, that he hasn't walked away, even clears his throat a little, maybe to let them know.

"You seem surprised," Pandora says after a moment, sipping their drink.

"I'm not certain any of this is what we might've expected when Staisy invited us to—" Bristol says, and Pandora waves their free hand.

"Drop it, it's okay, I know who you are. I can even guess why you're here, Lydia's aunt."

"I knew you'd blow our cover, Bits," Dolly says, grinning.

We all knew it would come to this, I don't say, but I might as well have, from the smile that crosses Pandora's face. "So what's the deal then?" I ask. "Why is everybody talking about infrastructure and projects?"

"Because my villainous scheme here, why I started this whole thing, created the chatbot—don't look surprised, I know it's not AI, you know it's not AI—was to make rich people actually fucking do something."

It's funny, this is kind of a villain monologue except, apparently, obviously, it isn't. "Pardon, make them do something?" Bristol asks. She hasn't touched her mimosa, I'm not sure she will. I'm not sure I will.

"These people aren't going to do politics or charity or anything on their own, their interests are always extremely selfish, and then they're *bored*. That's why they're always so petty and messy. So I decided, why not use my considerable abilities for *good*." They laugh, I assume at the looks on our faces, and tosses the rest of their drink back like it's a shot, setting the ringing glass on the coffee table. "They don't know what to do, I nudge them in the right direction. They want to be partying, we have a party right here. They like *feeling* good and having a purpose, but never, not in a million years, would've started a *charitable foundation* on their own, not one of them. Rich people used to do that all the time. It's lovely to self-aggrandize like that, make everybody thank you for the library, the hospital, the bridge."

"So why the charade, then, if you know who we are?" Bristol asks stiffly.

"Don't feel bad, it is Bits's fault that I know who you are. Your performance is impeccable, and lends credibility to those around you." Bristol purses her lips at being patronized like this, so extravagantly, but doesn't say anything. "No, I suppose I wanted to see what you would do, how far you would take it. And I can only assume what Lydia's aunt told you or had in store for me."

"She calls you a cult," Dolly says.

"She said that?" Pandora looks delighted. "She must really find us threatening. Which of course brings us to *your* specialty, which I do hope you won't exercise aboard ship."

"We weren't hired to kill you," Bristol says after a moment. We've never had a situation like this, there probably isn't a reason not to just have the cards on the table. They know who we are, we...well we're doing what we can.

"That's almost disappointing. I don't think I've actually had an assassination attempt yet, absurd as it would be. Oh yes, we must rid the world of Pandora, who has through their foundation helped hurricane-ravaged communities in America, brought solar power to overburdened grids in a number of countries worldwide, dug new wells in places with aquifers damaged by windmills...the list goes on."

"You should have a website," Dolly says dryly.

"But that would steal the thunder from the extremely rich and generous *individuals* who have started their initiatives. At my behest, but still." They look at their empty glass on the empty coffee table, and I watch their eyes move. Communicating in AR, I'm sure, it's a very obvious movement to me. Then they pick up a pack of cigarettes from the table, offer them around. Dolly takes one, then picks up a lighter and lights their cigarette first, then hers. "Thank you. But if not assassination, then what? How do you solve the puzzle of Lydia wanting to use her money for good, and her aunt wanting to maintain control of her empire?"

"It is quite the puzzle," Bristol agrees. "I don't suppose we could ask you to simply disinvite her?"

Pandora shakes their head. "No. I mean, you could ask, but I wouldn't."

"That is quite the quandary," Dolly says, and blows a smoke ring. I've seen her do that, then draw and shoot through it, but she doesn't. The ghost of those movements play out in my mind's eye, but the room is incredibly quiet. I'd think the walls were soundproofed, but I couldn't have heard Brent still in the hallway if they were.

"That is quite the party trick," Pandora is saying. They're very smug, sitting here with us like this. We should probably feel foolish, to have been caught playacting. Thinking we were infiltrating. This is very interesting, though. But it also means that it isn't really-really a cult, and Lydia isn't programmed, or at least not the way that we thought. That's kind of a shitty sell, though, isn't it? Now we need to stop this maybe-heiress from starting a humanitarian project? It's not like we're goody-goodies but come on here.

"Practice," Dolly says.

"Whatever made you think of this?" Bristol asks. She's still holding her glass, like it's a pretty accessory, and Pandora holds out their hand. Bristol passes them the drink. I put mine down on the table, but barely anybody even registers my movement.

"I woke up one day after years of using my powers, hacking, for fun and mischief and profit, and looked out on my empire of dirt, and thought to myself, what do I have left? Then I thought to myself, what did the real, or storied, Pandora have left." They look around at us, but this is the speech portion again, we aren't supposed to answer. "Hope. And then I thought, what if *I* could do that. What if I could give hope." Another theatrical pause. "I know, it sounds ridiculous, but I could have just stayed bored and disaffected and wasting my money on gadgets to fill the hole in my soul. But instead I called up Brayden and I told him I needed his yacht and then explained my bolt of lightning scheme and was so relieved when he agreed and now here we are."

"And Brent?"

"Oh they're married," They say dismissively. "And this yacht is a place where Brayden was spending his money. But this isn't solving your problem with Lydia, how do you solve a problem like *Lydia*? You'll forgive me for not breaking into song."

"It isn't necessary," Bristol agrees. "I suppose we'll continue to think it over?"

"While continuing to take advantage of my hospitality?" Pandora asks. "I'm not certain how much longer I'll tolerate that."

"It isn't as though you're about to maroon us on a desert island," Bristol says. "Do please be reasonable."

"No, but I can drop you at Morocco in a matter of hours, and I'm confident of the accommodations you'll find there," Pandora says with a smile, that Bristol matches.

"We might find that entirely suiting, thank you." There is the slightest of shifts in Pandora's expression and here is where they wonder if they had the upper hand on Bristol at all, actually. Everybody always ends up wondering eventually. I've watched her do it and could never replicate it myself. Bristol stands. "Shall we?"

"See you later?" Dolly says to Pandora, who drinks Bristol's mimosa and nods. "Thanks for the cigarette."

"You can keep the pack," they say. They aren't sullen, exactly, this was not a tremendous social defeat. But they expected it to be, with them as the victor. Maybe they expected us to sign up as well, and who can blame them. It's a compelling pitch. Making bored rich people do some good for once.

So our angle has changed. I'm remembering Bristol in Vietnam, after we gave the dog back, asking Dolly 'do you ever just want to feel *nice*?' with such a plaintive tone.

Chapter Thirteen

B rent is still standing in the hallway, and turns to say who knows what, except Dolly slugs back her mimosa that she's still holding and holds out the glass, and he almost reflexively raises the tray again to receive it. "You're one of the best bartenders I've met," she says, patting him on the shoulder as she passes, leading us down the hallway.

Brent doesn't say anything, but does look bemused, and goes into Pandora's cabin, closing the door. I guess we'll see how much time they give us.

Instead of going back topdeck, Dolly leads us through the corridors to our room. "Okay, how fucked are we?" she asks, and then laughs at the look on Bristol's face and holds up her hand. "Wait, no. I guess we're not fucked, really, either way. But if we wanna keep Pandora's gravy train going but pull Lydia, what are we gonna do?"

"Well we can hardly halt Pandora's...gravy train," Bristol says slowly. "It's indefensible, can you even *imagine*. People asking 'you did that to Pandora? Do you hate people having clean water.' This is dreadful, why did they have to be *doing good*."

"This is hilarious," Dolly says. Then a frown crosses her face and she pulls the pack of cigarettes out of her pocket and dumps it on the fold-out table. "Is this bugged?" she asks, and I laugh.

"Practically the whole yacht is." I look at them anyway. "The cigarettes aren't and the pack isn't."

"Okay, good." She lines them up and drops them back in the box, the remainder of the first one still burning slowly in the corner of her mouth. "These aren't just normal tobacco, the box says they're slow burn? Imagine the process of like, genetically engineerin' tobacco that burns slower than regular."

"Maybe they know the coffee people," I say distractedly, opening my message thread with Nautical Deborah. //So Pandora is the cult leader, just in the flesh. This is WILD.//

"Oh yeah maybe."

"What coffee people?" Bristol asks.

"Oh, Bits got coffee from a new convenience store we went to, that the can said—"

"Here," I say, getting out the other can.

//You MET Pandora??? What's the story?//

//They say they aren't running a cult, obviously it isn't a real AI (we know it isn't), and what's going on is every one of these bored rich people is doing like, cultural and humanitarian acts.//

//WHAT.//

//Pandora said they were a bored rich person and woke up one morning and were like 'what if I make this better?'//

//WHAT.//

//I know I know.//

//Do you...believe them?//

//I think so? I want to chase down the projects I just heard about this morning to verify.//

//So is that where the Pandora name comes from?//

//NO! Supposedly part of that wakeup was asking themself 'what do I have left.'//

//I've gotta say, when you said it was wild, I thought; how wild could it really be. But you don't exaggerate.//

//I try not to.//

"Bits. Bits. Bits. Bits." Dolly has been chanting this for...well not too long, that wasn't a very long conversation. Bristol is standing with her arms crossed. "Earth to Bitsy. Oh that sounds a lot like Heavens to Betsy, did your folks ever say that?"

"They did not," Bristol says.

"No."

"Regardless. We aren't Robin Hood, girls, but I'm hesitant to ruin something that seems to actually be quite good."

"Let me do some searching to make sure those projects are actually things that exist," I say. "It doesn't seem like everybody here could be paid actors but..."

"Nah, makes sense," Dolly says. "Everybody lies all the time."

"I don't suppose there's a website where all of these charitable actions are plainly gathered," Bristol says.

"It'd be real funny if there was, and Pandora's just waitin' for us to flail around."

"I'll look for that first, of course," I say. Because it does seem like Pandora in particular would think it was funny to let me chase my tail like that. And valid, really, it'd be embarrassing if I didn't even try to start with basic public knowledge, but also it's a really easy pitfall. When you're used to doing everything at a remove from a normal person's experience of technology and online things, you can forget the simplest ways to do things. "It'll be easier if I—"

"Hit the headset, yeah we know." Dolly tosses the coffee can back to me. "Me 'n' Bristol'll play poker or something."

"Hearts," Bristol says.

"You need four players for hearts," I say, pulling my headset up. I keep expecting the Ship to message me again, but I assume it won't anymore, now that everybody's dropping the act. I hope it won't anymore. I never wanted it to message me in the first place.

Of course there isn't just like, a 'Pandora's projects' website, but if I hadn't searched, of course there would've been. One by one, I match people who talked about things to contacts in Staisy's phone, and then track down the locations. One by one, they're real things that have happened and are ongoing. Somebody even did donate an ancestral home to a small town to be the library, that's a blast from the past. Even now, sometimes, libraries are the only places a person might be able to get internet access. It seems impossible, but of course, there are always places that get forgotten.

"They're real," I say, pushing my headset up.

"I'm still not certain if I'm relieved or disappointed," Bristol says. She's sitting on the little foldout chair by the little foldout table, phone in hand making The Dig noises.

"Well come on, let's think about how we go at this. What can we do, fake Lydia's death? Program the aunt to let her go? Kill the aunt?" Apparently, Dolly's kicked back on the upper bunk, smoking what I assume is another cigarette; the tobacco can't be *that* slow-burning.

"Dolly, we are not killing a higher up in organized crime."

"This time," she says cryptically, and I just blink at her.

"Surely we can appeal to the aunt's business sense?" Bristol asks.

"I mean, she hired us to do a thing that we aren't doing. Probably."

"Ultimately, she wants Lydia to stop being involved with this yacht," I say. My thoughts race ahead, and I pause to find the words, and they wait me out. "If Lydia's personal project could involve her aunt somehow, maybe we can make everybody happy?"

"Yeah, I'm sure she'll wanna get deeply mired in the family business in the name of doing good in the world."

"Money laundering," Bristol says. "Darlings, we don't need to know the particulars, we just need to be able to give Lydia compelling arguments to take home. If her philanthropic gestures also give her aunt a way of legitimizing less than clean funds, it could be the solution to their problems."

"That's so simple it just might work," Dolly says.

"Let's just hope Lydia agrees," I say.

"Oh yeah." Dolly kind of laughs, then swings to sitting, so her feet are dangling off the edge of her bunk. "She seemed to be feeling kinda positive towards Bristol, last we knew."

"This isn't a video game," I say, but video game mechanics come from somewhere, I guess. If only social interactions were actually that easy, but for people like Bristol, they are.

"No it ain't, but damn if Bristol doesn't still game the system somehow," Dolly says, laughing. "It's magic to watch, and she's so confused if it *doesn't* work."

"You recall I'm sitting right here, Dolly?"

"Yeah, I didn't forget." Dolly hops down, and sits next to me. "Okay, backup plan, is there any programming we can do?"

"So I'm going to repeat that this isn't a video game, I can't just program people at large. Not as quick and easy as we'd like, like I can't just send Lydia's aunt an activation phrase in her voicemail that'll let her just go ahead and do whatever while still getting us paid and not getting Pandora killed."

"Dang. I thought you could like, MKULTRA people at this point."

"No that's the one that they told everybody about so they could keep doing the real one," I say. Her leaps of logic are just dizzying sometimes.

"Oh, well fine then. You mentioned a virus before, though."

"I did, I did, but that was to get the hacker to lay off of Lydia with the AI cult stuff. Which isn't *really* what this is."

She glances at Bristol, who's looking at her phone again. "Bristol? This is your specialty, you got any input here?"

Bristol taps a few more things on her phone, and then looks up at us, smiling. "I thought I might just tell the truth."

"Oh shit, the truth," Dolly says. We look at each other, and start laughing.

"I never thought about the truth," I admit. "And who knows how she's going to take it."

"How would anybody take it? Hey this real cool person you think of as a mentor and/or leader is in mortal danger 'cause your aunt doesn't like you hangin' out with them. So let's manipulate your aunt into funding a project for you to launder her money. Everybody wins!"

"Well I won't say it quite like *that*," Bristol says, laughing. "Though I suppose you aren't far off. And were somebody to say such a thing to me, I'd certainly be angry with my hypothetical aunt, but willing to act to keep people safe."

"That's the nicest thing you've ever said about us, Bristles," Dolly says, nudging me with her elbow.

"I'm certain it isn't. I just don't always give compliments within earshot."

"Thats a shame, a little praise goes a long way."

Bristol leans in intently. "Are you coaching me?"

"Just givin' you a few pointers, yeah. The first couple are free, but after that it'll cost you."

"It's probably cost us already," I say. "Run through this again. Bristol goes out there and corrals Lydia and they have a heart to heart. She calls her aunt who's overjoyed she's coming home and wants to join the business and calls off the snipers. We get let off in Morocco and get paid. Is that everything?"

"Easy peasy," Dolly says. "What can go wrong?"

"Oh Dolly," Bristol sighs, and I can't help but wince a little. We've got an awful lot riding on one of the only female organized crime bosses going along with a slight manipulation.

"What? You're not superstitious."

"Even so." Bristol finishes on her phone and slides it into her caftan pocket. "I suppose I'll engage her in conversation throughout the day, and then after we've established a rapport, reveal our intent."

"Time's a-wastin, then. It's almost lunchtime." Dolly gets to her feet, slapping her pockets for cigarettes and lighter and I don't know what else, then stops. "Why does breakfast get the signature cocktail?"

"Pardon?"

"Everybody knows mimosas are for breakfast. Or brunch, I guess. But there's nothing else that's like 'oh yeah you have that at lunch' or 'this is for dinner.' Or maybe I don't know enough about cocktails."

"There's Death in the Afternoon," Bristol says thoughtfully. "And brandy tends to be after dinner."

"Yeah but that's also a cigars and men's clubs thing, which is anytime. I guess. Probably. Antiquated shit."

"People love traditions," I say. "And habits."

"And power and comfort and excitement," Bristol says. "But not too much excitement."

"There's always exceptions. So we'll leave you to it, Bitsy, and Bristol will salvage this thing for us and everything will go according to plan."

"Dolly," Bristol and I say at the same time, and we all laugh.

"Sorry, sorry, more whistling past graveyards." We look at her. "Yeah, no, I still don't think that's what that means."

"It's close, I guess," I say. When isn't Dolly relaxed, regardless of the situation? Almost never. Morocco. "Be careful."

"When aren't we?" Dolly says, winking and holding the door for Bristol, who sighs and shakes her head. "You too."

"I'll try," I say. If we consider this a done job, there's only so much trouble I can get in. But we really can't consider this a done job until we're off the boat and have the money in hand. So to speak.

I check Pandora's location on the ship; still in their cabin, that I can tell. Brent isn't there anymore, but they haven't physically left the space. I spend some time searching up Brent, to see what we're dealing with there. My faith in Dolly's capabilities is pretty much unshakeable, but more intel is always better. It seems like he was never enlisted, but he seems known in private security circles. Digging a little further, he was in a PMC for a few years, not a notable one, not a *problematic* one, but they kind of all are, aren't they? Like, the existence of private military forces isn't exactly what one might call healthy for society. That makes his enhancements make sense, though, and that makes his implied capacity as security make sense. Brayden isn't security, or even former law enforcement. No, his family has an older company that supplies things in the military and police circles, variant uniforms and protective equipment and flashy holsters and stuff. They're one of the places that has a subset of concealed carry clothing, like leggings and flannel shirts and things, to reel civilians in.

I have a brief thought that if Bristol carried a gun, she'd use concealed carry leggings, but no she wouldn't, Bristol doesn't typically wear leggings and she would never use something off the rack for such a potentially vital purpose. She'd definitely have somebody she knew to do things bespoke, like her tailor in Paris. Dolly's the one who uses everything off the rack and trades out equipment like breathing so she doesn't get too reliant on anything. Which might be why it took so long for her to make things legal with Butler.

I tap into the yacht systems again, carefully, quietly. Pandora doesn't expect anybody on board to be a hacker, I'm sure, which means anything I do that they detect will obviously lead back to me. But also it means that once I'm already in, things are pretty safe. Eventually, I find the programs that run the cooling systems for the file storage, and some more snooping gets me to the databases. Looking more closely now, I do think the darker forms in the code ocean are sharks, megalodons even, entirely out of scale to both the yacht and the rest of the ocean they're in. They must be the coded automated security response if somebody *is* caught snooping in the systems. Big and scary and distracting, to chomp onto your avatar and sever your connections to the code, while chasing your connection back to gain your physical location.

Stuff like that can't really physically hurt you, but the human brain is a funny thing. When we're in VR, the right code can fool us into thinking stuff is going physically wrong, at least for a little while. Something bad enough can put you into shock, or trigger a seizure or migraine if you're susceptible to those kinds of things. Even if you're not, sometimes; migraines weren't a part of my life before I got that black site virus. Nothing about Pandora makes me think their security would be anything less than the worst they could do to a perceived threat. Like, what kind of a person would rather that outsiders perceive your rolling yacht party as an AI cult, instead of a group of philanthropists? You'd think they would want attention, and they don't. Which makes me curious about who they're hiding from.

It isn't hard to make enemies, in this line of work. And I have no way to know, right this second, if Pandora is a rich person by birth or by business. But I've got at least a few hours, and I'm connected to the same wifi that all of their devices are, presumably, and that includes implants. People don't typically think about that, and especially if you're the monarch of all you survey, you wouldn't think about somebody checking the serial numbers on your corneal implants and tracking down the company and hacking their database to see where that batch was sold and then track down the distributor and then the subsequent clinic in London and the hack *their* database to see who received those implants.

Then I search up that family, which seems comfortably middle class. There are younger siblings still at home, though they no longer have to share a bedroom with their older sibling out of the house. Graduated from university, even, with a degree in economics. Their family thinks they work in Shanghai, something to do with the stock exchange. Something high powered and time consuming and stressful, though the hope is they'll make it home this Christmas, after missing a few.

I'm standing, digitally, outside the family home when Pandora walks up. They're in tall boots and a long tweedy coat now, instead of a caftan, as though it might be necessary to blend in on the physical street and not call undue attention from the residents within. //We used to feed the foxes at sunset,// they say. //Chicken and stuff.//

//We could never do that stateside. Rabies.//

//I know. The UK has managed to keep it out, still.// They turn to me; other than clothes, they look much how they did on the yacht this morning. Most people's avatars are just themselves lately, though trends come and go. I'm sure, soon enough, people will be anime characters or giant robots or barely-formed vapor clouds. And there's always furries. //There's no tragedy here. What I'm doing, who I am, isn't their fault. They aren't involved.//

//I was just thinking,// I say.

//Of Lydia and her aunt. Do you think my father would be upset, if he knew what I did? I think he just wouldn't understand, not want to sink the yacht.//

//Do parents tend to understand?// I don't think about mine often. Like Pandora, there's no tragedy there, except I *did* learn hacking at home. Mine don't think I might make it home for Christmas, though.

//Maybe not. It isn't really their role.//

//I guess it isn't.//

We stand looking at the house for a little while longer, and they really do seem to just be staying still for the moment, lost in thought. Not furiously messaging or coding or running programs or anything. //I suppose I should thank you for not just killing me.//

//That isn't really our style.//

//That's the impression that I got, from the stories. The ghost stories too.//

//It's hard to trust any of the stories, but I'm glad they get that right, at least.// Stories grow, whether you intentionally add to them or not. It's been tempting, to release false leads into the ecosystem, but also I don't want to actually cloud things and affect our reputations in a way like that. If we weren't working anymore, sure, but we've continued to take jobs for fun and profit. //We weren't hired to kill you, if that helps.//

//No, you were hired to solve the Lydia problem, which I presume will lead to that via other sources were you to be unsuccessful.//

//That is our assumption.//

Pandora smiles, so sadly. //Lydia has such promise. But I can't endanger myself, and the other members of our little club.//

//Why the AI deception?//

//Smoke and mirrors, of course. If I could create a "green AI" that's confined to the yacht and doesn't use a huge datacenter, that lends credibility to my idea of little projects like this. They're so careless with day to day affairs, but asking them for an *investment*, that makes them pause. Because it makes them look at themselves. It makes them think about the implications, what mark they are or are not leaving.//

//People don't like being confronted with themselves, if they weren't expecting to be.// Not like I'm an expert at introspection. People are people.

//They don't. So their expectations need setting up, their experience needs massaging.// Pandora shrugs. //I've been more successful with them than I might have expected. The fact that they're also trying to recruit on their own, without my nudging, is fantastic. It might mean that they'd carry on now, on their own, with this momentum.//

Dolly texts me. //Bits, we've gotta talk.//

//Good news, I hope,// I reply to her. Then I turn to Pandora. //I've got to go.//

//See you later.// They turn around and walk away, disappearing quickly around a corner. I log out, push my headset up.

"What's going on?" Both Dolly and Bristol are in the room. "What did Lydia say?"

"She is really very cross with her aunt," Bristol said. She's the kind of pink across the cheekbones that means she's been drinking a lot, or for a long time. An afternoon of umbrella drinks poolside at the yacht, getting herself in Lydia's good graces before dropping the bomb, I assume.

"But she took you seriously?"

"She did, and what a relief that was, I was utterly certain we'd have a terrible struggle with that."

"So then what's the story, where are we now?"

"Now Lydia's calling her aunt and telling her some boohoo she knows she's been making a terrible mistake running away from her responsibilities sorta story," Dolly says. "She doesn't want anybody here gettin' hurt, she's a good kid. Weird how right Pandora was."

"This whole thing has been a weird one," I say.

"So what've you been doin', other than not eating or drinkin' anything?" Dolly asks. She just can't understand that you don't *get* hungry or thirsty in VR, necessarily. Time passes differently. It's why the IV is so important, if you've got an actual immersion rig that you're using. With a headset, you're still aware of your body, but with enough hyperfocus, it's almost the same.

"I'll eat something soon," I say. I accept the bottle of water she shoves at me though. "I found out who Pandora is and where they're from. Just in case we needed it."

"Just like that?" Dolly asks, and I nod. "That's our girl!" she laughs. Bristol smiles.

"We know she's the best at what she does."

"Which is why she gets so mad when other people aren't as good. Well not mad, just disappointed I guess. Like the AI thing."

"I'm not disappointed the AI isn't real," I say, but is that true? Is that something that I still think, somehow, might really be real one day? Maybe. I don't know.

"Maybe not, but this didn't end up what you thought it was."

"It didn't end up to be what *any* of us thought," Bristol says. "I was certain, when they said AI cult, that it would be VR headsets and limp bodies on yoga mats as far as the eye could see. Within the constraints of the yacht, of course."

"Well that's an image," Dolly says, grimacing.

Chapter Fourteen

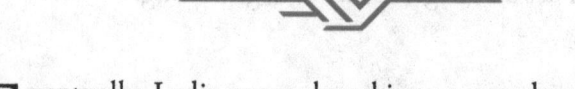

Eventually, Lydia comes knocking on our door. "I cannot believe her!" she says, stomping in past Dolly. "Hiring you to kidnap me! Like a child!"

"Hush, darling, she's only doing it because she cares for you and wants to protect you. Did your conversation go well?"

"She's welcoming me with open arms. I have access to her accounts, I can get a plane ticket home from anywhere in the world. I told her it might be Morocco?"

"It seemed like Pandora was gonna boot us in Morocco, yeah. You might not've been part of the us, but it might be safer to do that."

"Just like that?" I ask.

"Well. It ain't over til its over," Dolly says, right as Bristol asks

"Have you any idea how much longer before we reach the port?"

I pull up the map, then pull up the satellite access Nautical Deborah did to check our actual positioning and heading. "Well...it should be another couple of hours."

"Why'd you say it like that?" Dolly asks.

"Because we aren't actually heading towards Morocco." We hadn't been, actually, and if I'd thought about it for three seconds when she said something about not really marooning us, I would've remembered that we've been heading east, not west.

"Tell me they ain't double crossing us after we took the time to orchestrate savin' their life." Dolly says to the ceiling.

"I'm certain there's simply a closer port," Bristol says soothingly. "Why bring us all the way to Morocco when we're far closer to any number of other places? After all, it doesn't really behoove them to keep us on board if we have all discharged our duties."

"Yeah, yeah," Dolly says. "No reason to expect the worst."

"None at all," Bristol agrees. She pauses a moment, consciously, visibly. "Bits darling, would you say you discussed anything of particular note with Pandora?"

"I said that people didn't like being confronted with who they are, but that was after they already said the AI was to help the members think through the implications of having a consequential project, instead of just having careless lives."

"Well that's not too bad," Dolly says. "That's not like, world-crashing-down-around-your-ears bad."

"I didn't think so," I say, and then one of my Agency alerts pops up. "Oh for Christ's sake."

"What's the matter?" Bristol asks, but Dolly doesn't ask. She just waits, having gone very still.

"Somebody reported us on the Agency hotline," I say.

"Fucking Harding," Dolly spits. "I'm gonna kill him. Find him for me, I'm killing him."

"Hold that thought." I slide my headset back on as Lydia asks

"What's wrong? What's happening?"

"He disabled the hotline after your agreement," I say. "Well, he had it disabled. So I don't know if this is on him." 'Hotline' in this case meaning digital inbox that would accept voice, text, or data. Searching around in all the likely publicly-facing spaces, even when I previously found it there, either that page or post isn't there anymore, or if there is a link it 404s. I go to my Agency backdoor, scan it before interacting. Still the same as I left it, nobody on that side has touched it either. From the Agency's server side, there is a cached version of the hotline, not supposed to be interactible, but if somebody saved it, I guess they'd be able to. Clearly, they'd be able to, because when I trace those interactions, it leads me right back to Pandora. I chase other connections to that data, because there's a sudden cluster of new connections, all in the last fifteen minutes, and every last one leads be back to a phone on the yacht. "Okay, we need an exit strategy," I say. "Definitely not Harding's fault. Pandora cached the contact and every phone on the yacht made the call in the last little while"

"Butler better answer his phone," Dolly says.

"Bits, darling, isn't there any way to cancel these calls? After all, if Mr. Harding has agreed to leave us be, why would he respond to them instead of just deleting them?"

"They weren't going to him, nobody's monitoring that anymore, so it linked it to the main switchboard, and because the people monitoring *that* are seeing it come from a certain department's priority category, they..." I look again. "They think it's worth it to act on and sort out the mistake later, if it's a mistake. So we've got sort of an indeterminate amount of time between three and six hours. And because the response has already been forwarded and made contact with multiple humans, and *came from* multiple humans, I can't disappear it without it seeming even worse."

"But you said our Agency files are—"

"Not worth a damn, yeah, but I don't know what these calls say and don't think I've really got the leisure to unencrypt them right now." I look at Staisy's phone, but since I didn't set it up to record her calls, I can't play them back. Silly mistake, I hope it doesn't cost us too much.

Then Dolly is saying "Oh yeah I'm totally expectin' you to have storage units with fully fueled helis peppering the globe at strategic locations and I'm not askin' about a client I can steal from so we can just gracefully exfiltrate without me having to kill everybody on this damn yacht. I will explain what damn yacht at a later time. Thank you, yeah, forward it to Bits." She sighs. "That man, I swear."

I leave my headset on, and a few seconds later, Butler messages me a spreadsheet. I open it, skim it quick, then throw all the coordinates in the map app and find the closest one not in use. //Can I remote these?// I ask him.

//Sure can, here's the master key.// And messages me a packet. //So what the fuck?//

//Not right now, sorry.// The closest one is an hour and a half, I think. "Are we doing this from the yacht or are we cutting loose a lifeboat?"

"Yacht'll be easier," Dolly says. "For the helicopter. There's that big wide spot in the back that might as well be a helipad?"

"Understood." I plug in the flight plan, check its charge and condition as it spins up. The owner has it in a hangar, but of course has what amounts to a digital garage door opener in the console, and I hit that easily. The owner also doesn't seem to be home, this is probably just one of their properties. If I cover our tracks right, I can probably loop us right back there, we can park the thing, then drive off. "Okay. Ninety minutes." I pull the headset down so it hangs around my neck, it's more secure that way if we're going to be running around. Maybe we aren't, maybe Pandora just activated everybody's phones to send those calls.

"You think we got ninety minutes?" Dolly asks.

"Compared to Agency response, yeah that I know of," I say, frowning. There's a group text on Staisy's phone, but when I open it, the image doesn't make any sense to me. Oh. "Hey, Lydia, how much time has everybody spent talking to the AI?"

She shrugs; she might be pouting. "If they have a project and are at the right tier, half an hour each? When you add it all up?"

Plenty of time to have a virus, or posthypnotic suggestion, or whatever else you want to call it programmed into them, with or without implants. Bored brains can be very malleable, especially if they aren't really used to staring at a certain kind of technology for any length of time, and then spend time afterwards staring at something repetitive, like open water. Shit.

"Bits, darling, could you please share your insights with us?" Bristol asks tightly.

"I think it's possible Pandora has programmed everybody, and just sent them a trigger." Lydia starts to look at her phone, and Dolly bats it away, almost casually.

"Hey!"

"Sorry, but we don't need you sleep agent activatin' in the room here with us."

"I didn't get a text," she says. She's definitely pouting, and I can't help but laugh. She's pouting that she didn't get a group text triggering the people here to do...whatever they're going to do. Probably Brayden wouldn't have. Staisy is indoctrinated but he isn't.

"So I figure I gotta worry about Brent and Bradley, but everybody else is just quantity not quality," Dolly says. "And other'n those two, I haven't noticed anybody carrying. I guess there's no accountin' for sharpened hairpins, though," she says, winking at Bristol.

"I suppose there isn't," she says.

"Right." Dolly yanks out her suitcase, rummages, then pulls on a plate carrier. "Not the best if I gotta swim, but we'll burn that bridge when we get to it. Bitsy, you got protective gear?"

"My heavier dragonscale jacket," I say. She looks at me until I get it out of my suitcase and pull it on. At least the rooms of the yacht are air conditioned, I don't start sweating immediately. It's not as good as a plate carrier, but if what people are using are just handguns, it can handle a few shots.

"Bristles? That caftan ain't dragonscale, is it? Or that fancy silk? Did you hear about that, they gene edited some spiders and—"

"I do not have a spidersilk bulletproof caftan, no," Bristol says.

"You got...anything?" Dolly asks.

"One of my camisoles, in—" Dolly's already making a face and I know exactly why, but there's a noise outside that isn't the kind of noise you can talk over. It's a noise like, indeed, everybody on the yacht is coming down the little ladder stairs from the deck.

"Okay, taser time I guess?" She looks at me like I had a taser packed in my luggage for our commercial air flight. "Bits..."

"Give me a sec, let me get into the yacht system and..." I yank my headset up. I don't know what I'm going to do in the yacht system. Even if I thought the AI was real, it's been radio silent since Dolly placed that little USB for me, and doubly so since we talked to Pandora. If we hadn't done that, maybe I could've found a failsafe to implement. At least the yacht system is eyes and ears on most of the boat, and while not *everybody* is jostling and jammed together to get to our door, it's a lot of them. And the rest are doing things like dumping the life boats, which isn't an improvement, exactly. I run a search to see how many smartguns are on the yacht, which won't give me the real total number of guns on board but at least it's a start. Maybe predictably, there are only two smartguns, Brayden and Pandora. As for Brent, Dolly probably already has a better idea of what he has than I can guess.

I don't really know what Pandora did to these people. The right (or wrong, I guess) kind of programming can make people think they have greater physical acuity and adeptness than they really do. Like, their brains think they know kung fu, but their bodies can't really do it, just maybe approximate. Quantity, not quality, as Dolly says. Which is enough to be a big pain, especially if we don't really want to hurt these people. Which we don't, this isn't their fault. Well I don't, maybe Dolly feels less bad about it. I put a countdown for the helicopter ETA in her HUD, so she knows how long we have to hold out, and she sends me a plus sign in lieu of a thumbs up emoji. I don't know where she picked that up, but it's a fine shorthand.

Experimentally, I flash the yacht's emergency strobe lights, and watch to see if the people inside react. They frown, and cover their eyes, and shake their heads. They don't stop coming, but it slows them down. Not that they have all that far to go before clogging up the hallway entirely in front of our door, but even this smaller yacht is comically large. Not big enough to kill the remaining eighty six minutes, of course. Without taking my headset off, I say "I think if I flash the strobes and let the emergency tones go, that'll mess them up enough that we can leave the room, loop around, and get up on deck. The question is, do we want to do that?"

"The good thing about these little doors is I think they'll take a lot of pounding," Dolly says. "Maybe we want to wait until the helicopter's closer?"

"Whichever you girls choose," Bristol says.

"Do I get a vote?" Lydia asks.

"No," Dolly says. "We're more defensible here, and more defensible means I need to hurt less people before we blow this popsicle stand."

We wait, and the pounding does start. The hallway is also tight enough that only a few people can pound on the door at once, and they're shoving each other and tripping over each other to do it, sometimes falling and struggling to get up again, just a mass of caftans and flip flops and beachy waves. This would be funny if it wasn't kind of scary but also it's hard for it to be scary because it is funny.

These aren't zombies; periodically, people look around like they're wondering what they're doing, stop and take a few steps back. The problem is they take their phones out again, maybe to text Pandora and ask what's going on, and they get the signal again. So I spend a lot of time just bricking cell phones so that they can't continue to get the trigger, and a lot of those women *are* scared when they come back to themselves in the hallway like that, and shove and thrash until they get free so they can run off and lock themselves in their rooms.

Some people never check their phones again, though. Maybe they've always wanted to beat down a door in an angry mob, who can say. There are a lot of people who have always wanted to just go nuts. But after about twenty minutes of this, the door does audibly crack, and I pull my headset down again.

"I guess we're really in it now," Dolly says, grinning.

"I can trigger the fire suppression system but..."

"But if things escalate past a certain point, we're gonna want that workin', yeah." Dolly looks around the room like she's making sure she isn't forgetting something. "Grab what you can carry, I guess, but I'd encourage you not to bring anything."

"Dolly..." Bristol says, a little anxiously for her.

"Better out than in, Bristles. Just keep behind me if you can, stab 'em if you can't."

"Stab?" Lydia asks, as Bristol nods and pulls her hair pins out.

"We *do* like letting Dolly do the heavy lifting," she says.

"This is definitely a unique situation," Dolly says, and the door creaks, loudly. "Alright, taking out the door, you break right to go around like we discussed."

"Ready," I say. Fifty seven minutes.

Dolly rears back and kicks the door once in the middle, as hard as she can, boot planted flat, and the door breaks out, pushing the people in the hallway back. Bristol leads, Lydia follows, and I bring up the rear with my bag and Dolly's. I can always drop them, but also I know Dolly's got a first aid kit that I hope we won't need.

This way to the right is clear, and Bristol leads us to her room, grabs her bag with surprising swiftness, and we're moving again as Dolly catches up. "I'm desperately glad we traveled light this time," Bristol murmurs, as Dolly gives us a once over and then takes the lead. The hallway behind us is extremely quiet; I don't ask. Bristol doesn't ask. She isn't covered in blood and her hair is a mess, and if she wants to tell us about it later, she will. Good or bad, everything is Not Now. We've gotten out of plenty of tense situations, from people *trained* to be able to hurt us. I guess some of what makes this so fraught is that we don't want to badly hurt a bunch of brainwashed socialites, even if it is self defense.

We double back a couple of times when we hear more crowding up ahead, go through a billiards room with a nightmarish LED pool table and flashing karaoke setup, and duck into a sauna for another ten minutes, which is so hot after all that running that after six of those minutes I think that my heart might come out of the top of my head and my lungs might fall out, but I manage to keep all my organs in place until Dolly gives us the go ahead and we're back in the hallway and moving towards one of the stairways up to the deck.

Twenty minutes. Somehow. That was both the longest and shortest half hour of my life. I keep checking the helicopter as we go, and the helicopter keeps progressing towards us, unbothered. I keep swiping away messages from Will, and Nautical Deborah (after confirming Nautical Deborah wasn't offering me crucial information.)

We come out where the bell is, and at first, it looks like we might be alone on the deck. The sun is just starting to set, and the sky is all pink and orange and gold and then I remember that no, somebody has to be steering the boat, and it all clicks together in a matter of seconds, Brent stepping around from where he was hidden by where the instruments are, but not necessarily *hiding*. He doesn't have his gun out, at least, and Dolly looks relieved to see him, like finally somebody who both knows what's going on and knows what he's doing, so she doesn't have to hold herself back quite so completely.

He looks at her, and looks at me, then looks at Lydia and Bristol, a smile crossing his face. Dolly crosses the deck to meet him, and when she's about to make contact, he draws his gun and shoots Bristol.

Dolly doesn't stop herself, just slams right into him, and maybe for a second she thinks that he was trying to look like a quickdraw champion and shoot her but missed. But he drops the gun immediately, and once they're down and she's hit him once or twice and he hasn't hit her back, she stops, straddling him like a confused schoolyard bully.

Lydia is frozen in place, which is better than running in a direction, and I run to Bristol, who dropped immediately to the deck. The front of her caftan is all blood and she's's making a terrible wheezing noise, the most indelicate sound I've ever heard her make, and that doesn't really narrow down where he shot her and I'm trying to see where is wetter, darker, as I'm yanking open the zippers on Dolly's bag to get at the first aid kit, getting it stuck partway because my hands are panicking even if my brain isn't, and then I pick out the burnt-edged circular hole where the bullet went in, not quite in the middle of her chest, but up and to the right, and I grab a wad of gauze and press it there with my left hand while I get the foam cannister out with my right, I can't just let her bleed the whole time. I guess if it went all the way through, she's bleeding anyway, whether I put pressure here or not.

"Bristol, I'm going to plug up the wound with spray foam. It'll stop the bleeding, and it's got a painkiller in it. Then I'm going to inject you with one too. I'm sure this hurts more than anything ever has and I'm sorry, but the helicopter is less than ten minutes out and Dolly's going to know somewhere we can go to help you," I say. I don't know how much she can process what I'm saying, she's probably in shock already, if she's lucky. That'll help protect her from the pain. I hesitate, hating to let up on the pressure, then use it and fresh gauze to wipe the site, just to make sure I'm putting the nozzle in the right spot, and as I get it situated, Dolly comes and steadies me and we get the wound foamed and then she takes over, breaking open the syringe for the painkiller.

"Guess I still won't get to fly the helicopter on a job," she says tightly. "Can you handle it?"

"Yeah." I'll have to, anyway. Brent isn't where I saw him last, and Brayden isn't at the helm when I pass by to better see where I'm bringing the helicopter in. I decide, consciously, that I'm not going to worry about them anymore if Dolly isn't. I have a visual on the helicopter, and when I scan its dimensions and the back of the boat, they match up well enough that I'm able to set it down pretty easily. Maybe it's to Butler's credit, or Scooter or Meatball or whoever programs the remote driving on these. I don't have a lot of hands-on helicopter experience. Enough that I know I can do it, anyway.

I realize my hands are sticky and wipe them on my pants before realizing that won't be great in the long run but it's already done and the helicopter is here and waiting, finally, and I turn around to herd Lydia or help Dolly with Bristol. Lydia comes past me with our bags, though, ducking under the sweep of the blades like she was an old pro at this, and Dolly is right behind her carrying Bristol.

"Get in ahead and see if any of the seats'll lay down," she says. I tear my eyes away from Bristol's bone-pale face and get into the helicopter, pull at each of the seats until I find the one tucked away from the doors that does lay flat, and it looks like it has an IV bag hook molded into the wall over it, and if we had an IV to run that would be great but we don't. Dolly didn't wait for me to say yes or no, of course, she's been navigating getting them both on without jostling Bristol too much or putting her down again, until she's able to lay her in the seat and buckle her in. "Okay, call our guy in Dubai," she says.

"On it." That probably is closest, yeah. Closest of our known "guys," but if there's closer we need to take that option. I do call, though, and the receptionist, hearing something in my voice that I can't, puts me through to him immediately. It must have been end of day for him, but.

"Bits, where are you?"

"In the Mediterranean, near..." I look again, even though I already know. "Egypt, I guess."

"Much as I would love to have your business, my colleagues in Damascus are much closer," he says. "I'll send you the coordinates, and call them so that they're ready."

"Can we trust them?"

"As much as you can trust anybody," he says which, fair. "I vouch for them, if that's any comfort."

"It is, thank you." I get the helicopter into the air. "We're going to Damascus," I say in Dolly's earbuds and she grunts some kind of assent. I want to be able to help her, but this is the best way that I can help her, and I head east.

Epilogue

Lydia's on a train back to Russia hours and hours before we're able to get in and see Bristol. The whole time, Dolly paces the waiting room like a caged lion, venturing only as far away as the vending machines and the bathrooms, which are both just right there.

I can't really criticize her; while we should probably both try to sleep, I'm instead tracing Pandora and Bradley and Brent. They left the yacht adrift, taking a little speedboat to Alexandria, before getting on a plane to Johannesburg. I wait until they're hundreds of miles from anywhere, passing over Sudan, before I brick their plane.

I'm sure part of the delay in seeing Bristol is that once she regains sufficient consciousness to communicate, she absolutely doesn't *want* to be seen like this. I'm sure she also knows there's only so long she can keep Dolly out, though, before there are consequences, so eventually we're given the okay.

As soon as we walk into the room, she says "Darlings, moving forward we really *must* make sure nobody gets shot."

"Oh *now* we're deciding this, Bristol? Now?"

"Don't be mad at me, Dolly, you handle it so well every time, how was I to know this is what it's like?"

"This is like when people don't believe animals feel pain...okay you were supposed to reassure me that of course you knew."

Bristol smiles prettily, apologetically, and gestures at her little morphine remote button. "I'm so sorry, I'm simply unable to think, I can't cope with this."

"I agree with the new rule," I say cautiously.

"You're just sayin' that so it isn't ever your turn," Dolly fake grumbles.

About the Author

Jennifer R. Donohue grew up at the Jersey Shore and now lives in central New York with her husband and their Dobermans. She works at her local public library where she also facilitates a writing workshop. Her work has appeared in *Apex Magazine*, *Escape Pod*, *Fantasy*, *The Deadlands Fusion Fragment*, and elsewhere. Her debut novel, Exit Ghost, is available now. You can find her Bluesky @AuthorizedMusings.bsky.social, and you can subscribe to her Patreon for a new short story every month: https://www.patreon.com/JenniferRDonohue

Further work by Jennifer R. Donohue

Exit Ghost

The Drowned Heir

Between the Blood and the Sun

Burn Up in Victory

The Learn to Howl Trilogy

Learn to Howl

Baying the Moon

The Company of Wolves